EDITION

On rare occasions a single work establishes its author as a writer of major literary stature. Such was the case with Grace Paley's first book, *The Little Disturbances of Man,* published in 1959 to extraordinary critical acclaim.

This new book has all the warmth and vigor, the humor and perceptiveness of her first. It deals in the inimitable Paley manner with people in and out of love, with fathers and daughters, sons and mothers, husbands and wives, and passing strangers. For Grace Paley, the city is an extended village, and the intermeshing of ethnic types—Irish, Italian, Jewish, black—is an essential feature of her cityscape. *Enormous Changes at the Last Minute* surely confirms her standing as a masterful modern writer. Her wit, her fantastic ear for common speech, her brilliant imagery, and above all her insight into the affairs of ordinary human beings are simply unmatched.

GRACE PALEY is a New Yorker, and has been a typist, a housewife, and a writer most of her life. Currently, she teaches at Sarah Lawrence College.

# Enormous Changes at the Last Minute

STORIES BY

## Grace Paley

For
Jeannie Goldschmidt
And
Mike Kempton

A LAUREL EDITION
Published by
Dell Publishing Co., Inc.
1 Dag Hammarskjold Plaza
New York, New York 10017
Copyright © 1960, 1962, 1965, 1967, 1968,
1971, 1972, 1974 by Grace Paley
*The stories in this book appeared originally, some
in slightly different form, in the following magazines:*
*"Enormous Changes at the Last Minute,"*
*"Wants," "Debts," and "Distance" in* The Atlantic;
*"Faith in the Afternoon" in* The Noble Savage;
*"Gloomy Tune" and "Living" in* Genesis West;
*"Come On, Ye Sons of Art" in* Sarah Lawrence
Journal; *"Faith in a Tree" and "A Conversation
with My Father" in* New American Review;
*"Samuel," "The Burdened Man," and "The
Long-Distance Runner" in* Esquire; *"Politics" in* Win;
*"Northeast Playground" in* Ararat; *and
"The Immigrant Story" in* Fiction.
*The author is grateful to the editors of
these magazines for permission to reprint.*

Laurel ® TM 674623, Dell Publishing Co., Inc.
Reprinted by arrangement with Farrar, Straus & Giroux, Inc.
Printed in the United States of America
First Laurel printing—March 1975

*Everyone in this book is imagined
into life except the father.
No matter what story he has to live in,
he's my father, I. Goodside, M.D.,
artist, and storyteller.*
G. P.

# Contents

# Wants

I saw my ex-husband in the street. I was sitting on the steps of the new library.

Hello, my life, I said. We had once been married for twenty-seven years, so I felt justified.

He said, What? What life? No life of mine.

I said, O.K. I don't argue when there's real disagreement. I got up and went into the library to see how much I owed them.

The librarian said $32 even and you've owed it for eighteen years. I didn't deny anything. Because I don't understand how time passes. I have had those books. I have often thought of them. The library is only two blocks away.

My ex-husband followed me to the Books Returned desk. He interrupted the librarian, who had more to tell. In many ways, he said, as I look back, I attribute the dissolution of our marriage to the fact that you never invited the Bertrams to dinner.

That's possible, I said. But really, if you remember: first, my father was sick that Friday, then the children were born, then I had those Tuesday-night meetings, then the war began. Then we didn't seem to know them any more. But you're right. I should have had them to dinner.

I gave the librarian a check for $32. Immediately she

trusted me, put my past behind her, wiped the record clean, which is just what most other municipal and/or state bureaucracies will *not* do.

I checked out the two Edith Wharton books I had just returned because I'd read them so long ago and they are more apropos now than ever. They were *The House of Mirth* and *The Children,* which is about how life in the United States in New York changed in twenty-seven years fifty years ago.

A nice thing I do remember is breakfast, my ex-husband said. I was surprised. All we ever had was coffee. Then I remembered there was a hole in the back of the kitchen closet which opened into the apartment next door. There, they always ate sugar-cured smoked bacon. It gave us a very grand feeling about breakfast, but we never got stuffed and sluggish.

That was when we were poor, I said.

When were we ever rich? he asked.

Oh, as time went on, as our responsibilities increased, we didn't go in need. You took adequate financial care, I reminded him. The children went to camp four weeks a year and in decent ponchos with sleeping bags and boots, just like everyone else. They looked very nice. Our place was warm in winter, and we had nice red pillows and things.

I wanted a sailboat, he said. But you didn't want anything.

Don't be bitter, I said. It's never too late.

No, he said with a great deal of bitterness. I may get a sailboat. As a matter of fact I have money down on an eighteen-foot two-rigger. I'm doing well this year and can look forward to better. But as for you, it's too late. You'll always want nothing.

He had had a habit throughout the twenty-seven years of making a narrow remark which, like a plumber's snake, could work its way through the ear down the throat, halfway to my heart. He would then disappear, leaving me choking with equipment. What I mean is, I sat down on the library steps and he went away.

I looked through *The House of Mirth,* but lost interest. I felt extremely accused. Now, it's true, I'm short of requests and absolute requirements. But I do want *something*.

I want, for instance, to be a different person. I want to be the woman who brings these two books back in two weeks. I want to be the effective citizen who changes the school system and addresses the Board of Estimate on the troubles of this dear urban center.

I *had* promised my children to end the war before they grew up.

I wanted to have been married forever to one person, my ex-husband or my present one. Either has enough character for a whole life, which as it turns out is really not such a long time. You couldn't exhaust either man's qualities or get under the rock of his reasons in one short life.

Just this morning I looked out the window to watch the street for a while and saw that the little sycamores the city had dreamily planted a couple of years before the kids were born had come that day to the prime of their lives.

Well! I decided to bring those two books back to the library. Which proves that when a person or an event comes along to jolt or appraise me I *can* take some appropriate action, although I am better known for my hospitable remarks.

# Debts

A lady called me up today. She said she was in possession of her family archives. She had heard I was a writer. She wondered if I would help her write about her grandfather, a famous innovator and dreamer of the Yiddish theater. I said I had already used every single thing I knew about the Yiddish theater to write one story, and I didn't have time to learn any more, then write about it. There is a long time in me between knowing and telling. She offered a share of the profits, but that is something too inorganic. It would never rush her grandfather's life into any literature I could make.

The next day, my friend Lucia and I had coffee and we talked about this woman. Lucia explained to me that it was probably hard to have family archives or even only stories about outstanding grandparents or uncles when one was sixty or seventy and there was no writer in the family and the children were in the middle of their own lives. She said it was a pity to lose all this inheritance just because of one's own mortality. I said yes, I did understand. We drank more coffee. Then I went home.

I thought about our conversation. Actually, I owed nothing to the lady who'd called. It was possible that I did owe something to my own family and the families of my friends. That is, to tell their stories as simply as possible, in order, you might say, to save a few lives.

Because it was her idea, the first story is Lucia's. I tell it so that some people will remember Lucia's grandmother, also her mother, who in this story is eight or nine.

The grandmother's name was Maria. The mother's name was Anna. They lived on Mott Street in Manhattan in the early 1900's. Maria was married to a man named Michael. He had worked hard, but bad luck and awful memories had driven him to the Hospital for the Insane on Welfare Island.

Every morning Anna took the long trip by trolley and train and trolley again to bring him his hot dinner. He could not eat the meals at the hospital. When Anna rode out of the stone streets of Manhattan over the bridge to the countryside of Welfare Island, she was always surprised. She played for a long time on the green banks of the river. She picked wild flowers in the fields, and then she went up to the men's ward.

One afternoon, she arrived as usual. Michael felt very weak and asked her to lean on his back and support him while he sat at the edge of the bed eating dinner. She did so, and that is how come, when he fell back and died, it was in her thin little arms that he lay. He was very heavy. She held him so, just for a minute or two, then let him fall to the bed. She told an orderly and went home. She didn't cry because she didn't like him. She spoke first to a neighbor, and then together they told her mother.

Now this is the main part of the story:

The man Michael was not her father. Her father had

died when she was little. Maria, with the other small children, had tried to live through the hard times in the best way. She moved in with different, nearly related families in the neighborhood and worked hard helping out in their houses. She worked well, and it happened that she was also known for the fine bread she baked. She would live in a good friend's house for a while baking magnificent bread. But soon, the husband of the house would say, "Maria bakes wonderful bread. Why can't you learn to bake bread like that?" He would probably then seem to admire her in other ways. Wisely, the wife would ask Maria to please find another home.

One day at the spring street festival, she met a man named Michael, a relative of friends. They couldn't marry because Michael had a wife in Italy. In order to live with him, Maria explained the following truths to her reasonable head:

1. This man Michael was tall with a peculiar scar on his shoulder. Her husband had been unusually tall and had had a scar on his shoulder.
2. This man was redheaded. Her dead husband had been redheaded.
3. This man was a tailor. Her husband had been a tailor.
4. His name was Michael. Her husband had been called Michael.

In this way, persuading her own understanding, Maria was able to not live alone at an important time in her life, to have a father for the good of her children's character, a man in her bed for comfort, a husband to serve. Still and all, though he died in her arms, Anna, the child, didn't like him at all. It was a pity, because he had always called her "my little one." Every day she had

visited him, she had found him in the hallway waiting, or at the edge of his white bed, and she had called
out, "Hey, Zio, here's your dinner. Mama sent it. I
have to go now."

# Distance

You would certainly be glad to meet me. I was the lady who appreciated youth. Yes, all that happy time, I was not like some. It did not go by me like a flitting dream. Tuesdays and Wednesdays was as gay as Saturday nights.

Have I suffered since? No sir, we've had as good times as this country gives: cars, renting in Jersey summers, TV the minute it first came out, everything grand for the kitchen. I have no complaints worth troubling the manager about.

Still, it is like a long hopeless homesickness my missing those young days. To me, they're like my own place that I have gone away from forever, and I have lived all the time since among great pleasures but in a foreign town. Well, O.K. Farewell, certain years.

But that's why I have an understanding of that girl Ginny downstairs and her kids. They're runty, underdeveloped. No sun, no beef. Noodles, beans, cabbage. Well, my mother off the boat knew better than that.

Once upon a time, as they say, her house was the spit of mine. You could hear it up and down the air shaft, the singing from her kitchen, banjo playing in the parlor, she would admit it first, there was a tambourine in the bedroom. Her husband wasn't American. He had black hair—like Gypsies do.

And everything then was spotless, the kitchen was all inlay like broken-up bathroom tiles, pale lavender. Formica on all surfaces, everything bright. The shine of the pots and pans was turned to stun the eyes of company . . . you could see it, the mischievousness of that family home.

Of course, on account of misery now, she's always dirty. Crying crying crying. She would not let tap water touch her.

Five ladies on the block, old friends, nosy, me not included, got up a meeting and wrote a petition to Child Welfare. I already knew it was useless, as the requirement is more than dirt, drunkenness, and a little once-in-a-while whoring. That is probably something why the children in our city are in such a state. I've noticed it for years, though it's not my business. Mothers and fathers get up when they wish, half being snuggled in relief, go to bed in the afternoon with their rumpy bumpy sweethearts pumping away before 3 p.m. (So help me.) Child Welfare does not show its concern. No matter who writes them. People of influence, known in the district, even the district leader, my cousin Leonie, who put her all into electing the mayor, she doesn't get a reply if she sends in a note. So why should I, as I'm nothing but a Primary Day poll watcher?

Anyhow there are different kinds coming into this neighborhood, and I do not mean the colored people alone. I mean people like you and me, religious, clean, many of these have gone rotten. I go along with live and let live, but what of the children?

Ginny's husband ran off with a Puerto Rican girl who shaved between the legs. This is common knowledge and well known or I'd never say it. When Ginny heard that he was going around with this girl, she did it too, hoping to entice him back, but he got nauseated by her and that tipped the scales.

Men fall for terrible weirdos in a dumb way more and more as they get older; my old man, fond of me as he constantly was, often did. I never give it the courtesy of my attention. My advice to mothers and wives: Do not imitate the dimwit's girl friends. You will be damnfool-looking, what with your age and all. Have you heard the saying "Old dough won't rise in a new oven"?

Well, you know it, I know it, even the punks and the queers that have wiggled their way into this building are in on the inside dope. John, my son, is a constant attendant now at that Ginny's poor grubby flat. Tired, who can blame him, of his Margaret's shiny face all pitted and potted by Jersey smog. My grandchildren, of which I have close to six, are pale, as the sun can't have a chance through the oil in Jersey. Even the leaves of the trees there won't turn a greenish green.

John! Look me in the eye once in a while! What a good little twig you were always, we did try to get you out with the boys and you did go when we asked you. After school when he was eight or so, we got him into a bunch of Cub Scouts, a very raw bunch with a jawful of curse words. All of them tough and wild, but at attention when the master came among them. Right turn! You would've thought the United States Marines was in charge they was that accurate in marching, and my husband on Tuesday nights taught them what he recalled from being a sergeant. Hup! two, three, four! I guess is what he knew. But John, good as his posture was, when he come home I give him a hug and a kiss and "What'd you do today at Scouts, son? Have a parade, darling?"

"Oh no, Mother," says he. "Mrs. McClennon was collecting money the whole time for the district-wide picnic, so I just got the crayons and I drew this here picture of Our Blessed Mother," he says.

That's my John. And if you come with a Polaroid Land camera, you couldn't snap much clearer.

People have asked and it's none of their business: Why didn't the two of you (meaning Jack and me— both working) send the one boy you had left to college?

Well now to be honest, he would have had only grief in college. Truth: he was not bright. His father was not bright, and he inherited his father's brains. Our Michael was clever. But Michael is dead. We had it all talked over, his father and me, the conclusion we come to: a trade. My husband Jack was well established in the union from its early struggle, he was strong and loyal. John just floated in on the ease of recommendation and being related. We were wise. It's proved.

For now (this very minute) he's a successful man with a wonderful name in the building trade, and he has a small side business in cement plaques, his own beautiful home, and every kid of his dressed like the priest's nephew.

But don't think I'm the only one that seen Ginny and John when they were the pearls of this pitchy pigsty block. Oh, there were many, and they are still around holding the picture in the muck under their skulls, like crabs. And I am never surprised when they speak of it, when they try to make something of it, that nice-looking time, as though *I* was in charge of its passing.

"Ha," Jack said about twenty times that year, "she's a wild little bird. Our Johnny's dying . . . Watch her."

O.K. Wild enough, I guess. But no wilder than me

when *I* was seventeen, as I never told him, that whole year, long ago, mashing the grass of Central Park with Anthony Aldo. Why I'd put my wildness up against any wildness of present day, though I didn't want Jack to know. For he was a simple man . . . Put in the hours of a wop, thank God pulled the overtime of a decent American. I didn't like to worry worry worry him. He was kindness itself, as they say.

He come home 6 p.m. I come home 6:15 p.m. from where I was afternoon cashier. Put supper up. Seven o'clock, we ate it up and washed the dishes; 7:45 p.m. sharp, if there was no company present and the boy out visiting, he liked his pussy. Quick and very neat. By 8:15 he had showered every bit of it away. I give him his little whiskey. He tried that blabbermouth *Journal-American* for news of the world. It was too much. Good night, Mr. Raftery, my pal.

Leaving me, thank goodness, the cream of the TV and a cup of sweet wine till midnight. Though I liked the attentions as a man he daily give me as a woman, it hardly seemed to tire me as it exhausted him. I could stay with the Late Show not fluttering an eyelid till the very end of the last commercial. My wildness as a girl is my own life's business, no one else's.

Now: As a token for friendship under God, John'd given Ginny his high school G.O. pin, though he was already a working man. He couldn't of given her his union card (that never got customary), though he did take her to a famous dinner in honor of Klaus Schnauer; thirty-five years at Camillo, the only heinie they ever let into that American local; he was a disgusting fat-bottomed Nazi so help me, he could've turned you into a pink Commie, his ass, excuse me, was that fat. Well, as usual for the young-hearted gang, Saturday night went on and on, it give a terrible jolt to Sunday morning, and John staggered in to breakfast, not shaved or anything. (A man, husband, son, or lodger should be shaved at breakfast.) "Mother," he said, "I am going to ask Virginia to marry me."

"I told you so," said my husband and dropped the funnies on his bacon.

"You are?" I said.

"I am, and if God is good, she'll have me."

"No blasphemy intended," I said, "but He'll have to be off in the old country fishing if she says yes."

"Mother!" said John. He is a nice boy, loyal to friends and good.

"She'll go out with anyone at all," I said.

"Oh, Mother!" said John, meaning they weren't engaged, and she could do what she wanted.

"Go out is nothing," I said. "I seen her only last Friday night with Pete, his arm around her, going into Phelan's."

"Pete's like that, Mother," meaning it was no fault of hers.

"Then what of last Saturday night, you had to go to the show yourself as if there wasn't no one else in the Borough of Manhattan to take to a movie, and when you was gone I seen her buy two Cokes at Carlo's and head straight to the third floor to John Kameron's . . ."

"So? So?"

". . . and come out at 11 p.m. and *his* arm was around her."

"So?"

". . . and his hand was well under her sweater."

"That's not so, Mother."

"It *is* so, and tell me, young man, how you'll feel married to a girl that every wild boy on the block has

been leaning his thumbs on her titties like she was a
Carvel dairy counter, tell me that?"

"Dolly!" says Jack. "You went too far."

John just looked at me as red and dumb as a baby's
knees.

"I haven't gone far enough into the facts, and I'm
not ready to come out yet, and you listen to me,
Johnny Raftery, you're somebody's jackass, I'll tell you,
you look out that front window and I bet you if you got
yourself your dad's spyglass you would see some track
of your little lady. I think there are evenings she don't
get out of the back of that trailer truck parked over
there and it's no trouble at all for Pete or Kameron's
half-witted kid to get his way of her. Listen Johnny,
there isn't a grown-up woman who was sitting on the
stoop last Sunday when it was so damn windy that
doesn't know that Ginny don't wear underpants."

"Oh, Dolly," says my husband, and plops his head
into his hands.

"I'm going, Mother, that's libel, I'll have her sue you
for libel," dopey John starts to holler out of his tomato-
red face. "I'm going and I'll ask her and I love her
and I don't care what you say. Truth or lies, I don't
care."

"And if you go, Johnny," I said, calm as a dead fish,
my eyes rolling up to pray and be heeded, "this is what
I must do," and I took a kitchen knife, a bit blunt, and
plunged it at least an eighth of an inch in the fat of
my heart. I guess that the heart of a middle-aged lady
is jammed in deeper than an eighth of an inch, for I
am here to tell the tale. But some blood did come soon,
to my son's staring; it touched my nightie and spread
out on my bathrobe, and it was as red on my apron as
a picture in an Italian church. John fell down on his

knees and hid his head in my lap. He cried, "Mother, Mother, you've hurt yourself." My husband didn't say a word to me. He kept his madness in his teeth, but he told me later, Face it: the feelings in his heart was cracked.

I met Ginny the next morning in Carlo's store. She didn't look at me. Then she did. Then she said, "It's a nice day, Mrs. Raftery."

"Mm," I said. (It was.) "How can you tell the kind of day it is?" (I don't know what I meant by that.)

"What's wrong, Mrs. Raftery?" she said.

"Hah! wrong?" I asked.

"Well, you know, I mean, you act mad at me, you don't seem to like me this morning." She made a little laugh.

"I do. I like you a great deal," I said, outwitting her. "It's you, you know, you don't like Johnny. You don't."

"What?" she said, her head popping up to catch sight of that reply.

"Don't don't don't," I said. "Don't don't!" I hollered, giving Ginny's arm a tug. "Let's get out of here. Ginny, you don't like John. You'd let him court you, squeeze you, and he's very good, he wouldn't press you further."

"You ought to mind your business," says Ginny very soft, me being the elder (but with tears).

"My son is my business."

"No," she says, "he's his own."

"My son is my business. I have one son left, and he's my business."

"No," she says. "He's his own."

MY SON IS MY BUSINESS. BY LOVE AND DUTY.

"Oh no," she says. Soft because I am the older one, but very strong. (I've noticed it. All of a sudden they look at you, and then it comes to them, young people, they are bound to outlast you, so they temper up their icy steel and stare into about an inch away from you a lot. Have you noticed it?)

At home, I said, "Jack now, the boy needs guidance. Do you want him to spend the rest of his life in bed with an orphan on welfare?"

"Oh," said Jack. "She's an orphan, is she? It's just her mother that's dead. What has one thing to do with another? You're a pushy damn woman, Dolly. I don't know what use you are . . ."

What came next often happens in a family, causing sorrow at the time. Looking back, it's a speck compared to life.

For: Following this conversation, Jack didn't deal with me at all, and he broke his many years' after-supper habits and took long walks. That's what killed him, I think, for he was a habitual person.

And: Alongside him on one of these walks was seen a skinny crosstown lady, known to many people over by Tompkins Square—wears a giant Ukrainian cross in and out of the tub, to keep from going down the drain, I guess.

"In that case, the hell with you" is what I said. "I don't care. Get yourself a cold-water flat on Avenue D."

"Why not? I'll go. O.K.," said Jack. I think he figured a couple of weeks' vacation with his little cuntski and her color television would cool his requirements.

"Stay off the block," I said, "you slippery relic. I'll send your shirts by the diaper-service man."

"Mother," said poor John, when he noticed his dad's absence, "what's happening to you? The way you talk. To Dad. It's the wine, Mother. I know it."

"You're a bloated beer guzzler!" I said quietly. (People that drink beer are envious against the ones in favor of wine. Though my dad was a mick in cotton socks, in his house, we had a choice.)

"No, Mother, I mean you're not clear sometimes."

"Crazy, you mean, son. Huh? Split personality?"

"Something's wrong!" he said. "Don't you want Dad back?" He was nervous to his fingernails.

"Mind your business, he'll be back, it's happened before, Mr. Two-Weeks-Old."

"What?" he said, horrified.

"You're blind as a bat, Mr. Just Born. Where was you three Christmases ago?"

"What! But Mother! Didn't you feel terrible? Terrible! How'd you stand for him acting that way? Dad!"

"Now quit it, John, you're a damnfool kid. Sure I don't want to look at his dumb face being pleased. That'd kill."

"Mother, it's not right."

"Phoo, go to work and mind your business, sonny boy."

"It is my business," he said, "and don't call me sonny."

About two months later, John came home with Margaret, both of them blistered from Lake Hopatcong at ninety-four degrees. I will be fair. She was not yet ruined by Jersey air, and she was not too terrible looking, at least to the eye of a clean-minded boy.

"This is Margaret," he says. "She's from Monmouth, Jersey."

"Just come over on the *Queen Mary,* dear?" I asked for the joke in it.

"I have to get her home for supper. Her father's strict."

"Sure," I said, "have a Coke first."

"Oh, thank you so much," says Margaret. "Thank

you, thank you, thank you, Mrs. Raftery."

"Has she blood in her?" hollered Jack after his shower. He had come home by then, skinny and dissatisfied. Is there satisfaction anywhere in getting old?

John didn't inquire an O.K. of his dad or me, nor answer to nobody Yes or No. He was that age that couldn't live without a wife. He had to use this Margaret.

It was his time to go forward like we all did once. And he has. Number One: She is kept plugged up with babies. Number Two: As people nowadays need a house, he has bought one and tangled it around in Latin bushes. Nobody but the principal at Holy Redeemer High knows what the little tags on the twigs say. Every evening after hard work you can find him with a hose scrubbing down his lawn. His oldest kid is now fourteen and useless. The littlest one is four, and she reminds me of me with the flashiest eyes and a little tongue sharpened to a scrappy point.

"How come you never named one for *me*, Margaret?" I asked her straight in her face.

"Oh," she said, "there's only the two girls, Teresa, for my mother, and Cathleen, for my best sister. The very next'll be for you."

"What? Next! Are you trying to kill my son?" I asked her. "Why he has to be working nights as it is. You don't look well, you know. You ought to see a smart Jewish doctor and get your tubes tied up."

"Oh," she said, "never!"

I have to tease a little to grapple any sort of a reply out of her. But mostly it doesn't work. It is something like I am a crazy construction worker in conversation with fresh cement. Can there be more in the world like her? Don't answer. Time will pass in spite of her slow wits.

In fact it has, for here we are in the present, which
is happening now, and I am a famous widow babysitter
for whoever thinks I am unbalanced but within
reason. I am a grand storybook reader to the little
ones. I read like an actress, Joan Crawford or Maureen
O'Sullivan, my voice is deeper than it was. So I do
make a little extra for needs, though my Johnny sees to
the luxuries I must have. I won't move away to strangers. This is my family street, and I don't need to.

And of course as friendship never ends, Johnny
comes twice a week for his entertainment to Ginny.
Ginny and I do not talk a word, though we often pass.
She knows I am right as well as victorious. She's had
it unusually lovely (most people don't)—a chance to
be some years with a young fellow like Blackie that
gave her great rattling shivers, top to bottom, though
it was all cut off before youth ended. And as for my
Johnny, he now absolutely has her as originally planned
and desired, and she depends on him in all things. She
requires him. Her children lean on him. They climb
up his knees to his shoulder. They cry out the window
for him, *John, John,* if his dumb Margaret keeps him
home.

→ It's a pity to have become so right and Jack's off
stalking the innocent angels.

I wait on the stoop steps to see John on summer
nights, as he hasn't enough time to visit me and Ginny
both, and I need the sight of him, though I don't
know why. I like the street anyway, and the hot night
when the ice-cream truck brings all the dirty kids and
the big nifty boys with their hunting-around eyes. I put
a touch of burgundy on my strawberry ice-cream cone
as my father said we could on Sunday, which drives
these sozzle-headed ladies up the brown brick wall, so
help me Mary.

Now, some serious questions, so far unasked:

What the devil is it all about, the noisiness and the speediness, when it's no distance at all? How come John had to put all them courtesy calls into Margaret on his lifelong trip to Ginny? Also, Jack, what was his real nature? Was he for or against? And that Anthony, what *did* he have in mind as I knuckled under again and again (and I know I was the starter)? He did not get me pregnant as in books it happens at once. How come the French priest said to me, crying tears and against his order, "Oh no, Dolly, if you are *enceinte* (meaning pregnant), he will certainly marry you, poor child, now smile, poor child, for that is the Church's promise to infants born." To which, how come, tough and cheery as I used to be, all I could say before going off to live and die was: "No, Father, he doesn't love me."

# Faith
# in the
# Afternoon

As for you, fellow independent thinker of the Western Bloc, if you have anything sensible to say, don't wait. Shout it out loud right this minute. In twenty years, give or take a spring, your grandchildren will be lying in sandboxes all over the world, their ears to the ground, listening for signals from long ago. In fact, kneeling now on the great plains in a snootful of gray dust, what do you hear? Pigs oinking, potatoes peeling, Indians running, winter coming?

Faith's head is under the pillow nearly any weekday midnight, asweat with dreams, and she is seasick with ocean sounds, the squealing wind stuck in its rearing tail by high tide.

That is because her grandfather, scoring the salty sea, skated for miles along the Baltic's icy beaches, with a frozen herring in his pocket. And she, all ears, was born in Coney Island.

Who are her antecedents? Mama and Papa of course. Her environment? A brother and a sister with their own sorrow to lead by the nose out of this life. All together they would make a goddamn quadruped bilingual hermaphrodite. Even so, proving their excellence, they bear her no rancor and are always anxious to see her, to see the boys, to take the poor fatherless boys to a picnic with their boys, for a walk, to an ocean, glad to

say, we saw Mama in the Children of Judea, she sends
love . . . They never say snidely, as the siblings of others might, It wouldn't hurt you to run over, Faith, it's
only a subway ride . . .

Hope and Faith and even Charles—who comes glow-
ering around once a year to see if Faith's capacity for
survival has not been overwhelmed by her susceptibility
to abuse—begged their parents to reconsider the decision to put money down and move into the Children
of Judea. "Mother," said Hope, taking off her eye-
glasses, for she did not like even that little window of
glass to come between their mother and herself. "Now,
Mother, how will you make out with all those *yentas?*
Some of them don't even speak English." "I have spok-
en altogether too much English in my life," said Mrs.
Darwin. "If I really liked English that much, I would
move to England." "Why don't you go to Israel?"
asked Charles. "That would at least make sense to people." "And leave you?" she asked, tears in her eyes at
the thought of them all alone, wrecking their lives on
the shoals of every day, without her tearful gaze at-
tending.

When Faith thinks of her mother and father in any
year, young or impersonally aged, she notices that they
are squatting on the shore, staring with light eyes at the
white waves. Then Faith feels herself so damply in the
swim of things that she considers crawling Channels
and Hellesponts and even taking a master's degree in
education in order to exult at last in a profession and
get out of the horseshit trades of this lofty land.

Certain facts may become useful. The Darwins
moved to Coney Island for the air. There was not
enough air in Yorkville, where the grandmother had
been planted among German Nazis and Irish bums by

Faith's grandfather, who soon departed alone in blue pajamas, for death.

Her grandmother pretended she was German in just the same way that Faith pretends she is an American. Faith's mother flew in the fat face of all that and, once safely among her own kind in Coney Island, learned real Yiddish, helped Faith's father, who was not so good at foreign languages, and as soon as all the verbs and necessary nouns had been collected under the roof of her mouth, she took an oath to expostulate in Yiddish and grieve only in Yiddish, and she has kept that oath to this day.

Faith has only visited her parents once since she began to understand that because of Ricardo she would have to be unhappy for a while. Faith really is an American and she was raised up like everyone else to the true assumption of happiness.

No doubt about it, squinting in any direction she is absolutely miserable. She is ashamed of this before her parents. "You should get help," says Hope. "Psychiatry was invented for people like you, Faithful," says Charles. "My little blondie, life is short. I'll lay out a certain amount of cash," says her father. "When will you be a person," says her mother.

Their minds are on matters. Severed Jerusalem; the Second World War still occupies their arguments; peaceful uses of atomic energy (is it necessary altogether?); new little waves of anti-Semitism lap the quiet beaches of their accomplishment.

They are naturally disgusted with Faith and her ridiculous position right in the middle of prosperous times. They are ashamed of her willful unhappiness.

All right! Shame then! Shame on them all!

*     *     *

That Ricardo, Faith's first husband, was a sophisticated man. He was proud and happy because men liked him. He was really, he said, a man's man. Like any true man's man, he ran after women too. He was often seen running, in fact, after certain young women on West Eighth Street or leaping little fences in Bedford Mews to catch up with some dear little pussycat.

He called them pet names, which generally referred to certain flaws in their appearance. He called Faith Baldy, although she is not and never will be bald. She is fine-haired and fair, and regards it as part of the lightness of her general construction that when she gathers her hair into an ordinary topknot, the stuff escapes around the contour of her face, making her wisp-haired and easy to blush. He is now living with a shapely girl with white round arms and he calls her Fatty.

When in New York, Faith's first husband lives within floating distance of the Green Coq, a prospering bar where he is well known and greeted loudly as he enters, shoving his current woman gallantly before. He introduces her around—hey, this is Fatty or Baldy. Once there was Bugsy, dragged up from the gutter where she loved to roll immies with Russell the bartender. Then Ricardo, to save her from becoming an old tea bag (his joke), hoisted her on the pulpy rods of his paperbacked culture high above her class, and she still administers her troubles from there, poor girl, her knees gallivanting in air.

Bugsy lives forever behind the Horney curtain of Faith's mind, a terrible end, for she used to be an ordinarily reprehensible derelict, but by the time Ricardo had helped her through two abortions and one lousy winter, she became an alcoholic and a whore for money. She soon gave up spreading for the usual rewards, which are an evening's companionship and a weekend of late breakfasts.

Bugsy was before Faith. Ricardo agreed to be Faith's husband for a couple of years anyway, because Faith in happy overindulgence had become pregnant. Almost at once, she suffered a natural miscarriage, but it was too late. They had been securely married by the state for six weeks when that happened, and so, like the gentleman he may very well be, he resigned himself to her love—a medium-sized, beefy-shouldered man, Indian-black hair, straight and coarse to the fingers, lavender eyes—Faith is perfectly willing to say it herself, to any good listener: she loved Ricardo. She began indeed to love herself, to love the properties which, for a couple of years anyway, extracted such heartwarming activity from him.

Well, Faith argues whenever someone says, "Oh really, Faithy, what do you mean—love?" She must have loved Ricardo. She had two boys with him. She had them to honor him and his way of loving when sober. He believed and often shouted out loud in the Green Coq, that Newcastle into which he reeled every night, blind with coal, that she'd had those kids to make him a bloody nine-to-fiver.

Nothing, said Faith in those simple days, was further from her mind. For her public part, she had made reasoned statements in the playground, and in the A & P while queued up for the cashier, that odd jobs were a splendid way of making out if you had together agreed on a substandard way of life. For, she explained to the ladies in whom she had confided her entire life, how can a man know his children if he is always out working? How true, that is the trouble with children today, replied the ladies, wishing to be her friend, they never see their daddies.

* * *

"Mama," Faith said, the last time she visited the Children of Judea, "Ricardo and I aren't going to be together so much any more."

"Faithy!" said her mother. "You have a terrible temper. No, no, listen to me. It happens to many people in their lives. He'll be back in a couple of days. After all, the children . . . just say you're sorry. It isn't even a hill of beans. Nonsense. I thought he was much improved when he was here a couple of months ago. Don't give it a thought. Clean up the house, put in a steak. Tell the children be a little quiet, send them next door for the television. He'll be home before you know it. Don't pay attention. Do up your hair something special. Papa would be more than glad to give you a little cash. We're not poverty-stricken, you know. You only have to tell us you want help. Don't worry. He'll walk in the door tomorrow. When you get home, he'll be turning on the hi-fi."

"Oh, Mama, Mama, he's tone deaf."

"Ai, Faithy, you have to do your life a little better than this."

They sat silently together, their eyes cast down by shame. The doorknob rattled. "My God, Hegel-Shtein," whispered Mrs. Darwin. "Ssh, Faith, don't tell Hegel-Shtein. She thinks everything is her business. Don't even leave a hint."

Mrs. Hegel-Shtein, president of the Grandmothers' Wool Socks Association, rolled in on oiled wheelchair wheels. She brought a lapful of multicolored wool in skeins. She was an old lady. Mrs. Darwin was really not an old lady. Mrs. Hegel-Shtein had organized this Active Association because children today wear cotton socks all winter. The grandmothers who lose heat at their extremities at a terrible clip are naturally more sensitive to these facts than the present avocated generation of mothers.

"Shalom, darling," said Mrs. Darwin to Mrs. Hegel-Shtein. "How's tricks?" she asked bravely.

"Aah," said Mrs. Hegel-Shtein. "Mrs. Essie Shifer resigned on account of her wrists."

"Really? Well, let her come sit with us. Company is healthy."

"Please, please, what's the therapy value if she only sits? Phooey!" said Mrs. Hegel-Shtein. "Excuse me, don't tell me that's Faith. Faith? Imagine that. Hope I know, but this is really Faith. So it turns out you really have a little time to see your mother . . . What luck for her you won't be busy forever."

"Oh, Celia, I beg you, be quiet," Faith's mortified mother said. "I must beg you. Faith comes when she can. She's a mother. She has two little small boys. She works. Did you forget, Celia, what it was like in those days when they're little babies? Who comes first? The children . . . the little children, they come first."

"Sure, sure, first, I know all about first. Didn't Archie come first? I had a big honor. I got a Christmas card from Florida from Mr. and Mrs. First. Listen to me, foolish people. I went by them to stay in the summer place, in the woods, near rivers. Only it got no ventilation, the whole place smells from termites and the dog. Please, I beg him, please, Mr. First, I'm a old woman, be sorry for me, I need extra air, leave your door open, I beg, I beg. No, not a word. Bang, every night eleven o'clock, the door gets shut like a rock. For a ten-minute business they close themselves up a whole night long.

"I'm better off in a old ladies' home, I told them. Nobody there is ashamed of a little cross ventilation."

Mrs. Darwin blushed. Faith said, "Don't be such a clock watcher, Mrs. Hegel-Shtein."

Mrs. Hegel-Shtein, who always seemed to know Faith better than Faith knew Mrs. Hegel-Shtein, said, "All right, all right. You're here, Faithy, don't be lazy. Help out. Here. Hold it, this wool on your hands, your mama will make a ball." Faith didn't mind. She held the wool out on her arms. Mrs. Darwin twisted and turned it round and round. Mrs. Hegel-Shtein directed in a loud voice, wheeling back and forth and pointing out serious mistakes. "Gittel, Gittel," she cried, "it should be rounder, you're making a square. Faithy, be more steadier. Move a little. You got infantile paralysis?"

"More wool, more wool," said Mrs. Darwin, dropping one completed ball into a shopping bag. They were busy as bees in a ladies' murmur about life and lives. They worked. They took vital facts from one another and looked as dedicated as a kibbutz.

The door to Mr. and Mrs. Darwin's room had remained open. Old bearded men walked by, thumbs linked behind their backs, all alike, the leftover army of the Lord. They had stuffed the morning papers under their mattresses, and because of the sorrowful current events they hurried up to the Temple of Judea on the sixth floor, from which they could more easily communicate with God. Ladies leaned on sticks stiffly, their articulations jammed with calcium. They knocked on the open door and said, "Oi, busy . . ." or "Mrs. Hegel-Shtein, don't you ever stop?" No one said much to Faith's mother, the vice-president of the Grandmothers' Wool Socks Association.

Hope had warned her: "Mother, you are only sixty-five years old. You look fifty-five." "Youth is in the heart, Hopey. I feel older than Grandma. It's the way I'm constituted. Anyway Papa is practically seventy, he deserves a rest. We have some advantage that we're young enough to make a good adjustment. By the time we're old and miserable, it'll be like at home here." "Mother, you'll certainly be an object of suspicion, an interloper, you'll have enemies everywhere." Hope had been sent to camp lots of years as a kid; she knew a thing or two about group living.

Opposite Faith, her mother swaddled the fat turquoise balls in more and more turquoise wool. Faith swayed gently back and forth along with her outstretched wool-wound arms. It hurt her most filial feelings that, in this acute society, Mrs. Hegel-Shtein should be sought after, admired, indulged . . .

"Well, Ma, what do you hear from the neighborhood?" Faith asked. She thought they could pass some cheery moments before the hovering shadow of Ricardo shoved a fat thumb in her eye.

"Ah, nothing much," Mrs. Darwin said.

"Nothing much?" asked Mrs. Hegel-Shtein. "I heard you correctly said nothing much? You got a letter today from Slovinsky family, your heart stuck in your teeth, Gittel, you want to hide this from little innocent Faith. Little baby Faithy. Ssh. Don't tell little children? Hah?"

"Celia, I must beg you. I have reasons. I must beg you, don't mix in. Oh, I must beg you, Celia, not to push any more, I want to say nothing much on this subject."

"Idiots!" Mrs. Hegel-Shtein whispered low and harsh.

"Did you really hear from the Slovinskys, Mama, really? Oh, you know I'm always interested in Tessie. Oh, you remember what a lot of fun Tess and I used to have when we were kids. I liked her. I never didn't like her." For some reason Faith addressed Mrs. Hegel-Shtein: "She was a very beautiful girl."

"Oh, yeh, beautiful. Young. Beautiful. Very old

story. Naturally. Gittel, you stopped winding? Why?
The meeting is tonight. Tell Faithy all about Slovinsky,
her pal. Faithy got coddled from life already too much."

"Celia, I said shut up!" said Mrs. Darwin. "Shut
up!"

(Then to all concerned a short dear remembrance
arrived. A policeman, thumping after him along the
boardwalk, had arrested Mr. Darwin one Saturday
afternoon. He had been distributing leaflets for the
Sholem Aleichem School and disagreeing reasonably
with his second cousin, who had a different opinion
about the past and the future. The leaflet cried out in
Yiddish: "Parents! A little child's voice calls to you,
'Papa, Mama, what does it mean to be a Jew in the
world today?' " Mrs. Darwin watched them from the
boardwalk bench, where she sat getting sun with a
shopping bag full of leaflets. The policeman shouted
furiously at Mr. and Mrs. Darwin and the old cousin,
for they were in an illegal place. Then Faith's mother
said to him in the Mayflower voice of a disappearing
image of life, "Shut up, you Cossack!" "You see," said
Mr. Darwin, "to a Jew the word 'shut up' is a terrible
expression, a dirty word, like a sin, because in the beginning, if I remember correctly, was the word! It's a
great assault. Get it?")

"Gittel, if you don't tell this story now, I roll right
out and I don't roll in very soon. Life is life. Everybody today is coddlers."

"Mama, I want to hear anything you know about
Tess, anyway. Please tell me," Faith asked. "If you
don't tell me, I'll call up Hope. I bet you told her."

"All stubborn people," said Mrs. Darwin. "All right.
Tess Slovinsky. You know about the first tragedy,
Faith? The first tragedy was she had a child born a
monster. A real monster. Nobody saw it. They put it

in a home. All right. Then the second child. They went right away ahead immediately and they tried and they had a second child. This one was born full of allergies. It had rashes from orange juice. It choked from milk. Its eyes swoll up from going to the country. All right. Then her husband, Arnold Lever, a very pleasant boy, got a cancer. They chopped off a finger. It got worse. They chopped off a hand. It didn't help. Faithy, that was the end of a lovely boy. That's the letter I got this morning just before you came."

Mrs. Darwin stopped. Then she looked up at Mrs. Hegel-Shtein and Faith. "He was an only son," she said. Mrs. Hegel-Shtein gasped. "You said an only son!" On deep tracks, the tears rolled down her old cheeks. But she had smiled so peculiarly for seventy-seven years that they suddenly swerved wildly toward her ears and hung like glass from each lobe.

Faith watched her cry and was indifferent. Then she thought a terrible thought. She thought that if Ricardo had lost a leg or so, that would certainly have kept him home. This cheered her a little, but not for long.

"Oh, Mama, Mama, Tessie never guessed what was going to happen to her. We used to play house and she never guessed."

"Who guesses?" screamed Mrs. Hegel-Shtein. "Archie is laying down this minute in Florida. Sun is shining on him. He's guessing?"

Mrs. Hegel-Shtein fluttered Faith's heart. She rattled her ribs. She squashed her sorrow as though it were actually the least toxic of all the world's great poisons.

However, the first one to live with the facts was Mrs. Hegel-Shtein. Eyes dry, she said, "What about Brauns? The old Braun, the uncle, an idiot, a regular Irgunist, is here."

"June Braun?" Faith asked. "My friend June Braun?

From Brighton Beach Avenue? That one?"

"Of course, only, that isn't so bad," Mrs. Darwin said, getting into the spirit of things. "Junie's husband, an engineer in airplanes. Very serious boy. Papa doesn't like him to this day. He was in the movement. They bought a house in Huntington Harbor with a boat, a garage, a garage for the boat. She looked stunning. She had three boys. Brilliant. The husband played golf with the vice-president, a goy. The future was golden. She was active in everything. One morning they woke up. It's midnight. Someone uncovers a little this, a little that. (I mentioned he was in the movement?) In forty-eight hours, he's blacklisted. Good night Huntington Harbor. Today the whole bunch live with the Brauns in four rooms. I'm sorry for the old people."

"That's awful, Mama," Faith said. "The whole country's in a bad way."

"Still, Faith, times change. This is an unusual country. You'll travel around the world five times over, you wouldn't see a country like this often. She's up, she's down. It's unusual."

"Well, what else, Mama?" Faith asked. June Braun didn't sorrow her at all. What did June Braun know about pain? If you go in the dark sea over your head, you have to expect drowning cheerfully. Faith believed that June Braun and her husband whatever-his-name-could-be had gone too deeply into the air pocket of America whence all handouts come, and she accepted their suffocation in good spirit.

"What else, Mama? I know, what about Anita Franklin? What about her? God, was she smart in school! The whole senior class was crazy about her. Very chesty. Remember her, she got her period when she was about nine and three quarters? Or something like that. You knew her mother very well. You were always in cahoots about something. You and Mrs. Franklin. Mama!"

"You sure you really want to hear, Faithy, you won't be so funny afterward?" She liked telling these stories now, but she was not anxious to tell this one. Still she had warned Faith. "All right. Well, Anita Franklin. Anita Franklin also didn't guess. You remember she was married way ahead of you and Ricardo to a handsome boy from Harvard. Oh, Celia, you can imagine what hopes her mother and her father had for her happiness. Arthur Mazzano, you know, Sephardic. They lived in Boston and they knew such smart people. Professors, doctors, the finest people. History-book writers, thinking American people. Oh, Faithy darling. I was invited to the house several times, Christmas, Easter. I met their babies. Little blondies like you were, Faith. He got maybe two Ph.D.'s, you know, in different subjects. If someone wanted to ask a question, on what subject, they asked Arthur. At eight months their baby walked. I saw it myself. He wrote articles for Jewish magazines you never heard of, Celia. Then one day, Anita finds out from the horse's mouth itself, he is fooling around with freshmen. Teenagers. In no time it's in the papers, everybody in court, talking talking talking, some say yes, some no, he was only flirting, you know the way a man flirts with youngsters. But it turns out one of the foolish kids is pregnant."

"Spanish people," said Mrs. Hegel-Shtein thoughtfully. "The men don't like their wives so much. They only get married if it's a good idea."

Faith bowed her head in sorrow for Anita Franklin, whose blood when she was nine and three quarters burst from her to strike life and hope into the busy heads of all the girls in the fifth and sixth grades. Anita Franklin, she said to herself, do you think you'll make it all alone? How do you sleep at night, Anita Franklin, the sexiest girl in New Utrecht High? How is it these days, now you are never getting laid any more by clever Arthur Mazzano, the brilliant Sephardic Scholar and Lecturer? Now it is time that leans across you and not handsome, fair Arthur's mouth on yours, or his intelligent Boy Scouty conflagrating fingers.

At this very moment, the thumb of Ricardo's hovering shadow jabbed her in her left eye, revealing for all the world the shallowness of her water table. Rice could have been planted at that instant on the terraces of her flesh and sprouted in strength and beauty in the floods that overwhelmed her from that moment on through all the afternoon. For herself and Anita Franklin, Faith bowed her head and wept.

"Going already, Faith?" her father asked. He had poked his darling birdy head with poppy pale eyes into the sun-spotted room. He is not especially good-looking. He is ugly. Faith has often thanked the Germ God and the Gene Goddess and the Great Lords of All Nucleic Acid that none of them look like him, not even Charles, to whom it would not matter, for Charles has the height for any kind of face. They all look a little bit Teutonish, like their grandmother, who thinks she's German, just kind of light and even-featured, with Charles inclining to considerable jaw. People expect decision from Charles because of that jaw, and he has learned to give it to them—the wit of diagnosis, then inescapable treatment, followed by immediate health. In fact, his important colleagues often refer their wives' lower abdominal distress to Charles. Before he is dead he will be famous. Mr. Darwin hopes he will be famous soon, for in that family people do not live long.

Well, this popeyed, pale-beaked father of Faith's peered through the room into the glassy attack of the afternoon sun, couldn't focus on tears, or bitten lips for that matter, but saw Faith rise to look for her jacket in the closet.

"If you really have to go, I'll walk you, Faithy. Sweetheart, I haven't seen you in a long time," he said. He withdrew to wait in the hallway, well out of the circle of Mrs. Hegel-Shtein's grappling magnetism.

Faith kissed her mother, who whispered into her damp ear, "Be something, don't be a dishrag. You have two babies to raise." She kissed Mrs. Hegel-Shtein, because they had been brought up that way, not to hurt anyone's feelings, particularly if they loathed them, and they were much older.

Faith and her father walked through the light-green halls in silence to the life-giving lobby, where rosy, well-dressed families continued to arrive in order to sit for twenty minutes alongside their used-up elders. Some terrible political arguments about Jews in Russia now were taking place near the information desk. Faith paid no attention but moved toward the door, breathing deeply. She tried to keep her father behind her until she could meet the commitments of her face. "Don't rush, sweetheart," he said. "Don't rush, I'm not like these old cockers here, but I am no chicken definitely."

Gallantly he took her arm. "What's the good word?" he asked. "Well, no news isn't bad news, I hope?"

"So long, Chuck!" he called as they passed the iron gate over which, in stunning steel cursive, a welder had inscribed *The Children of Judea*. "Chuckle, chuckle," said her father, grasping her elbow more firmly, "what a name for a grown-up man!"

She turned to give him a big smile. He deserved an enormous smile, but she had only a big one available.

"Listen, Faithy, I wrote a poem, I want you to hear. Listen. I wrote it in Yiddish, I'll translate it in my head:

> Childhood passes
> Youth passes
> Also the prime of life passes.
> Old age passes.
> Why do you believe, my daughters,
> That old age is different?

"What do you say, Faithy? You know a whole bunch of artists and writers."

"What do I say? Papa." She stopped stock-still. "You're marvelous. That's like a Japanese Psalm of David."

"You think it's good?"

"I love it, Pa. It's marvelous."

"Well . . . you know, I might give up all this political stuff, if you really like it. I'm at a loss these days. It's a transition. Don't laugh at me, Faithy. You'll have to survive just such events some day yourself. Learn from life. Mine. I was going to organize the help. You know, the guards, the elevator boys—colored fellows, mostly. You notice, they're coming up in the world. Regardless of hopes, I never expected it in my lifetime. The war, I suppose, did it. Faith, what do you think? The war made Jews Americans and Negroes Jews. Ha ha. What do you think of that for an article? 'The Negro: Outside In at Last.' "

"Someone wrote something like that."

"Is that a fact? It's in the air. I tell you, I'm full of ideas. I don't have a soul to talk to. I'm used to your mother, only a funny thing happened to her, Faithy. We were so close. We're still friendly, don't take me the wrong way, but I mean a funny thing, she likes to be with the women lately. Loves to be with that insane, persecution, delusions-of-grandeur, paranoical Mrs. Hegel-Shtein. I can't stand her. She isn't a woman men can stand. Still, she got married. Your mother says, Be polite, Gersh; I am polite. I always loved the ladies to a flaw, Faithy, but Mrs. Hegel-Shtein knocks at our room at 9 a.m. and I'm an orphan till lunch. She has magic powers. Also she oils up her wheelchair all afternoon so she can sneak around. Did you ever hear of a wheelchair you couldn't hear coming? My child, believe me, what your mother sees in her is a shady mystery. How could I put it? That woman has a whole bag of spitballs for the world. And also a bitter crippled life."

They had come to the subway entrance. "Well, Pa, I guess I have to go now. I left the kids with a friend."

He shut his mouth. Then he laughed. "Aaah, a talky old man . . ."

"Oh no, Pa, not at all. No. I loved talking to you, but I left the kids with a friend, Pa."

"I know how it is when they're little, you're tied down, Faith. Oh, we couldn't go anywhere for years. I went only to meetings, that's all. I didn't like to go to a movie without your mother and enjoy myself. They didn't have babysitters in those days. A wonderful invention, babysitters. With this invention two people could be lovers forever.

"Oh!" he gasped, "my darling girl, excuse me . . ." Faith was surprised at his exclamation because the tears had come to her eyes before she felt their pain.

"Ah, I see now how the land lies. I see you have trouble. You picked yourself out a hard world to raise a family."

"I have to go, Pa."

"Sure."

She kissed him and started down the stairs.

"Faith," he called, "can you come soon?"

"Oh, Pa," she said, four steps below him, looking up, "I can't come until I'm a little happy."

"Happy!" He leaned over the rail and tried to hold her eyes. But that is hard to do, for eyes are born dodgers and know a whole circumference of ways out of a bad spot. "Don't be selfish, Faithy, bring the boys, come."

"They're so noisy, Pa."

"Bring the boys, sweetheart. I love their little goyish faces."

"O.K., O.K.," she said, wanting only to go quickly. "I will, Pa, I will."

Mr. Darwin reached for her fingers through the rail. He held them tightly and touched them to her wet cheeks. Then he said, "Aaah . . ." an explosion of nausea, absolute digestive disgust. And before she could turn away from the old age of his insulted face and run home down the subway stairs, he had dropped her sweating hand out of his own and turned away from her.

# Gloomy
# Tune

There is a family nearly everybody knows. The children of this family are named Bobo, Bibi, Doody, Dodo, Neddy, Yoyo, Butch, Put Put, and Beep.

Some are girls and some are boys.

The girls are mean babysitters for mothers. The boys plan to join the army.

The two oldest mean babysitters go out to parties a lot. Sometimes they jerk people off. They really like to.

They are very narrow-minded. They never have an idea. But they like to be right. They never listen to anyone else's ideas.

One after another, Dodo, Neddy, Yoyo, and Put Put got the sisters at the school into a state. The sisters had to give up on them and they got dumped where they belonged for being fresh: right in the public school.

Around four years old, they began to be bad by cursing, and they went on from there.

First they said ass, then bitch, then fuckn bitch. Then when they got a little bigger, motherfuckn bitch, and so on, but I don't like to say.

The sister was strict first, very angry and cold as ice. You can hardly blame her. She wasn't ever a mother, had children, or done anything like that.

She was strict and she was right to be strict. Of

course, no strictness at home is the real reason for bold-
ness and freshness.

Then the sister wanted to try kindness too. She spoke
very kindly. She took all her own time to sit, especially
with Neddy who was so cute, and she helped him in
arithmetic.

She was good. She taught Yoyo checkers. But his
mind wasn't on it. When kindness was useless, she had
to say in each case, As far as our school is concerned,
sorry. God help you, you must go. You don't deserve
a wonderful education. There's so many waiting behind
you just for the chance.

She went to see their mother, who was doing the
wash in a terrible hurry before going to work. I don't
know what it is, sister, the mother said. They get in
with the tough kids moving in the neighborhood, you
know the ones I mean.

Oh, oh, said the sister who was tired of always hearing mean gossip, oh, oh, whose children are we, dear
missus, every single one of us?

The mother didn't say a word. Because she knew the
sister couldn't understand a thing. Now, the sister didn't
know what it was like to live next door to all kinds.

Ah listen sister dear, said the mother, could you keep
an eye on Put Put? Bobo's gonna be in any minute to
watch out for him. I been late four times already on
that job. I better go so help me. What the hell's holding that girl up? You don't know what's gone on in the
high schools today. Sister, I know your time ain't your
own.

Now you better hurry, said sister, getting to perspire
in the place. Oh I am sorry about Neddy. And Yoyo.
Oh, how I wish we could hold them.

Of course public school being what it is, they didn't
improve. Got worse and began to say, Go suck your

father's dick. I don't think they really understood what
they were saying.

They never stole. They had a teeny knife. They
pushed people on the slides and knocked them all over
the playground. They wouldn't murder anyone I think.

They cursed a lot and pushed back a lot. Someone
usually pushed them first or cursed them first. They had
a right to curse back or push back.

One day, not later than was expected, Chuchi Gomez
slipped in an olive-oil puddle left by a lady whose bottle broke. She picked up the bottle pieces, but didn't
do a thing about the oil. I wouldn't know what to do
about the oil either.

Chuchi said, turning to Yoyo in back of him, Why
you push me bastard?

Who pushed you, you dope? said Yoyo.

You dumb bastard, you push me. I feel over here on
my shoulder, you push me.

Aah go on, I didn push you, said Yoyo.

I seen you push me. I feeled you push me. Who you
think you go around pushin. Bastard.

Who you callin bastard, you big mouth. You call me
a bastard?

Yeh, said Chuchi, the way I figure, you a motherfuckn bastard.

You call me a motherfuckn bastard?

Yeh, you. I call you that. You see this here oil. That's
what I call you.

Then Yoyo was so mad because he and Chuchi had
plans to go to the dock for eels Sunday. Now he
couldn't have any more plans with Chuchi.

So he hollered, You better not say my mother's
name, you hear me, Chuchi stinking Gomez. Your
whole family's a fuckn bitches starting with your father and mother and Eddie and Ramon and Lilli and all

the way the whole bunch and your gramma too.

Then he picked up a board with two nails in it and clonked Chuchi on the shoulder.

That isn't such a bloody place, but with the oil and blood and all, if you got a little vinegar, you could of pickled Chuchi.

Then Chuchi yelped and screamed, Don you murder me. And he ran home to his gramma who was in charge of him.

His gramma lay right down in bed when she saw Chuchi and hollered, I don wanna see no more in this bad country. Kill me, I beg you, somebody.

No, no, said Chuchi, don't feel so bad Gramma. It wasn't my fault. He started it. You better take me to the clinic.

His gramma was disgusted that she couldn't even lie down a minute in her age to holler a little. But she had to take Chuchi to the clinic. They gave him a couple of shots for nail poisoning.

Well you see how Yoyo got well known for using a knife. The people from Greenwich House to Hudson Guild know his name. He is bold and hopeless.

In school he gets prayed for every day by all the kids, girls or boys.

# Living

Two weeks before Christmas, Ellen called me and said, "Faith, I'm dying." That week I was dying too.

After we talked, I felt worse. I left the kids alone and ran down to the corner for a quick sip among living creatures. But Julie's and all the other bars were full of men and women gulping a hot whiskey before hustling off to make love.

People require strengthening before the acts of life.

I drank a little California Mountain Red at home and thought—why not—wherever you turn someone is shouting give me liberty or I give you death. Perfectly sensible, thing-owning, Church-fearing neighbors flop their hands over their ears at the sound of a siren to keep fallout from taking hold of their internal organs. You have to be cockeyed to love, and blind in order to look out the window at your own ice-cold street.

I really was dying. I was bleeding. The doctor said, "You can't bleed forever. Either you run out of blood or you stop. No one bleeds forever."

It seemed *I* was going to bleed forever. When Ellen called to say she was dying, I said this clear sentence: "Please! I'm dying too, Ellen."

Then she said, "Oh, oh, Faithy, I didn't know." She said, "Faith, what'll we do? About the kids. Who'll take care of them? I'm too scared to think."

I was frightened too, but I only wanted the kids to stay out of the bathroom. I didn't worry about them. I worried about me. They were noisy. They came home from school too early. They made a racket.

"I may have another couple of months," Ellen said. "The doctor said he never saw anyone with so little will to live. I don't want to live, he thinks. But Faithy, I do, I do. It's just I'm scared."

I could hardly take my mind off this blood. It's hurry to leave me was draining the red out from under my eyelids and the sunburn off my cheeks. It was all rising from my cold toes to find the quickest way out.

"Life isn't that great Ellen," I said. "We've had nothing but crummy days and crummy guys and no money and broke all the time and cockroaches and nothing to do on Sunday but take the kids to Central Park and row on that lousy lake. What's so great, Ellen? What's the big loss? Live a couple more years. See the kids and the whole cruddy thing, every cheese hole in the world go up in heat blast firewaves . . ."

"I want to see it all," Ellen said.

I felt a great gob making its dizzy exit.

"Can't talk," I said. "I think I'm fainting."

Around the holly season, I began to dry up. My sister took the kids for a while so I could stay home quietly making hemoglobin, red corpuscles, etc., with no interruption. I was in such first-class shape by New Year's, I nearly got knocked up again. My little boys came home. They were tall and handsome.

Three weeks after Christmas, Ellen died. At her funeral at that very neat church on the Bowery, her son took a minute out of crying to tell me, "Don't worry Faith, my mother made sure of everything. She took care of me from her job. The man came and said so."

"Oh. Shall I adopt you anyway?" I asked, wondering, if he said yes, where the money, the room, another ten minutes of good nights, where they would all come from. He was a little older than my kids. He would soon need a good encyclopedia, a chemistry set. "Listen Billy, tell me the truth. Shall I adopt you?"

He stopped all his tears. "Why thanks. Oh no. I have an uncle in Springfield. I'm going to him. I'll have it O.K. It's in the country. I have cousins there."

"Well," I said, relieved. "I just love you Billy. You're the most wonderful boy. Ellen must be so proud of you."

He stepped away and said, "She's not anything of anything, Faith." Then he went to Springfield. I don't think I'll see him again.

But I often long to talk to Ellen, with whom, after all, I have done a million things in these scary, private years. We drove the kids up every damn rock in Central Park. On Easter Sunday, we pasted white doves on blue posters and prayed on Eighth Street for peace. Then we were tired and screamed at the kids. The boys were babies. For a joke we stapled their snowsuits to our skirts and in a rage of slavery every Saturday for weeks we marched across the bridges that connect Manhattan to the world. We shared apartments, jobs and stuck-up studs. And then, two weeks before last Christmas, we were dying.

# Come On,
# Ye Sons
# of Art

The way Zandakis comes on smiling! says Jerry Cook, biggest archbishopric in New Jersey in the palm of his hand; shy saints, relics all kinds; painted monks blessed by the dumbest ladies, bawling madonnas.

Everywhere in America, he says, giving Kitty a morning hour, New Jersey and Long Island man is looking at God and about Him, says Jerry Cook, I dream.

Oh, he says further, turning over to stare, as far as money is concerned, I love the masters. Baby, admit it, the masters are scientists. They add and they multiply. After that they water and they weigh. They're artists. They lay low. They are smiling in a hot bath and the whole damn East Coast leather-goods industry grows up out of the crap in their teeth. They are bulldozers. Two Jew experts in any regular recession can mash twenty-five miserable Syrians. One old Greek, he's half asleep, he puts his marble shoulder on fifty Jews. Right away a hundred thousand plastic briefcases get dumped into bargain bins of Woolworth, New York. Don't mention the Japanese.

Why not? asked Kitty.

Never, said Jerry Cook, no matter to whom, I never mention the Japanese.

Who Cook worked for was Gladstein. There were

billings up and down 46, 1, 22 for maybe 285,000 all in secular goods. If you see a cheap wallet in Orange County, Jerry Cook put it there.

But what is Gladstein compared to Zandakis? Zandakis, so help me, he is touched by the pinky of the Holy Spirit and the palm of Eastern Orthodox. You can see Gladstein from here, put-putting behind that greasy genius, giving out 20-by-60 Flushing building lots at swamp-bottom prices to his wife's nephews. Dumbhead Gladstein is not even afraid of Taiwan. He is on the high seas, but he thinks it's Central Park Lake. He holds a dance for the showoff of it all once a month out on deck, which is a twentieth-floor penthouse over Broadway and Seventh Avenue, the black tidewaters. In the war he turned old maid's sweater buttons into golden captain's buttons and internal security exploded in him—to his fingertips—like a dumdum, and now he includes the switchboard girls in his party, the key-punch girls, the dictaphone girls, the groovy bookkeepers, he even includes Jerry Cook, very democratic.

Only Karl Marx, the fly in the ointment, knows how come Zandakis turned on Gladstein just when his in-laws loved him the most and ground him into drygoods. In a minute 325,000 little zippered real-leather ladies' change purses were rammed into the digestion of starving Mrs. Lonesome, the Jersey Consumer.

Envy of Zandakis and pain about Gladstein made Jerry Cook bitter.

Business! he said. You think I'm in business. You think Gladstein is business—with his Fulton Street molds and his Florentine bookmarks. You think tobacco pouches is business! He bit his nails.

No! But diamonds! Kitty, say it to me, say diamonds, he said.

O.K. Diamonds, she said.

Well, that's better. That's business. I call that business. I should go right to diamonds. Kitty, it's a fact, old bags, you slip them the salami nice, they buy anything. That's what I hear everywhere.

Don't go into diamonds, said Kitty.

Oh yes, he said, giving the pillow a rabbit punch. I know you Kitty. You're one of that crowd. You're the kind thinks the world is round. Not like my sister, he said. Not Anna Marie. She knows the real shape. She lived, Anna Marie. What did she have, when she was a kid, what'd my father give her, a little factory to begin with, embroidery, junk, but she's shrewd and crooked and she understands. My two brothers are crooked. Crooked, crooked. They have crooked wives. The only one is not crooked, the one who is straight and dumb like you Kitty—Kitty, Kitty—he said, dragging her to him for a minute's kiss—is her husband, Anna Marie's. He was always dumb and straight, but they have got him now, all knotted up, you wouldn't unravel him if you started in August.

Kitty, with your personality, you should be in some business. Only for a year, to buy and sell, it's a gimmick.

But they are thieves. Baby. My brothers. Oh listen they worked for famous builders one time. They're known. Planit Brothers. Millions of dollars. You don't know reality. Kitty, you're not in contact, if you don't realize what a million dollars is. (It is one and six zeroes running after.) That was the Planit Corner Cottages, Every Cottage a Corner Plot. How they did it was short blocks. Every penny they stole from the government. So? What's the government for? The people? Kitty, you're right. And Planit Brothers is people, a very large family.

Four brothers and three sisters, they wouldn't touch birth control with a basement beam. Orthodox. Constructive fucking. Builders, baby.

Meanwhile my brother Skippy mentions $40,000. Come on! What is $40,000. Ask the bank. Go to the bank. They tear up $40,000. They jump up and down on it. They spit on it. They laugh. You want to sink in one stick of a foundation, the cost is maybe $12,000. It disappears into the ground. Into the ground and farewell.

But listen Kitty. Anna Marie is shrewd. SHE HAS A HEAD, hollered Jerry Cook, leaping out of bed and rapping his own with his pointing forefinger. Anna Marie, she tells my brothers, while you're working for Planit, take something, for God's sakes. Take a little at a time. Don't be greedy. Don't be dumb. The world is an egg, jackasses, suck it. It's pure protein, you won't get fat on your heart. You might get psychosomatic, but you won't get fat.

Jerry Cook sighed. He fell back into bed, exhausted, and talked softly against Kitty's soft breast. Take something, Anna Marie said, sinks, boilers, stoves, washing machines, lay it up, lay it up. Slowly. Where, my brothers ask, should we lay up? Where? they asked. It was my brothers. I wasn't there. I'm not in on it. Kitty, I don't know why, he said sadly. I'm crooked too.

Sure you are, said Kitty.

You guys make me puke, said Anna Marie. I took care of all that already. She had really done that. Taken care of where to stack it away. She had gone and bought a warehouse. In an auction. Where else do you get one?

Tie! Tie bid! the auctioneer hollers. A quarter of a million, screams one sharpie. At the same simultaneous minute, a quarter of a million, screams the other sharpie. Ha! The auctioneer bangs the gavel. Bang! Tie bid!

I never heard of that, said Kitty.

You sheltered yourself, said Jerry Cook. My sister says to him, Marv. You look like a pig half the time. You look like a punk, you don't look like an auctioneer. What do you look like? Name it. Schlep, he says. Laughs. Right-o. Schlep. Listen, Marv, give me this warehouse for 70,000. I'll slip you back 7 and an Olds. Beautiful car, like a horse, she says. I know your wife's a creep, she don't put out. I'll fix you up nice. You don't deserve to look such a bum. Right away he's grateful. Hahahah, breathes hard. He thinks he's getting laid. What? My sister? Anna Marie. Not her. No. She wouldn't do that. Never. Still, that's what he thinks.

My brothers say, Sure, introduce him. A nice brunette, a blonde, redhead, something from Brooklyn. You know? Not Anna Marie. Too smart. I ain't in the roast-beef business, Skippy, she says to my brother Skippy . . .

Because she's not! Anna Marie could be in any business she chose. She learned from my mother and father. They knew. But what did she do when her time came to do? She looked up at the sky. It was empty. Where else could she put her name and fame? Oh Anna Marie. High risers! she said. Oh, she could choose to be in anything. She could sell tushies in Paris. She could move blondes in Sweden. Crooked, he said, his heart jumping like a fool in his throat. He sat up straight. High risers!

On the East Side, on the North Side. Democratic. She put one up in Harlem. She named it. She digs spades. Not what you think, Kitty. Digs them. She sees it coming, Anna Marie. She sees who she's dealing with in ten years, twenty years. Life is before her. You have to watch *The New York Times.* The editorial section, who they're for. THEN do business.

HARRIET TUBMAN TOWERS, that's what I name you, twenty-seven stories. Looks out over Central Park, Madison Avenue, the Guggenheim Museum. If you happen to live in the back, the Harlem River, bridges, the South Bronx, and a million slaves.

A colonial power I planted here, she says. She missed the boat though, naming it that way. She's putting up another one more west, she already got the name for it, black, like onyx halls, a sphinx fountain, a small Cleopatra's needle in the playground, you know, for the kids to climb on. EGYPT, she calls it. They like that. She doesn't build, Anna Marie, till she got the name. In the Village, what do you see, for instance: Cézanne, Van Gogh, St. Germain . . . Jerks, transient tenancy, concessions, vacancies in the second year . . . She reads the papers there, *The Villager,* the *Voice.* She sniffs. Anna Marie is shrewd. Quiet, she looks the contractor in the face. FRANZ KLINE. And she is oversubscribed the day after they paste the plans up.

You ought to go into business, Kitty. You're not shrewd. But you're loving and you got tolerance. There's a place for that. You wouldn't be a millionaire, but you'd get out of this neighborhood. What have your kids got here, everywhere they go, shvartzes, spics and spades. Not that I got a thing against them, but who needs the advance guard.

Kitty put her finger over his lips. Ssh, she said. I am tolerant and loving.

Come on, Kitty. Did you like the mockies right out of steerage? They stunk. Those Yids, you could smell them a precinct away. Beards like a garlic farm. What can you do . . . Europe in those days . . . Europe was backwards. Today you could go into a gym with the very same people. People forget today about the backwardness of Europe.

But listen, Kitty, once my sister decided about high risers . . .

Who? said Kitty. Decided what?

My sister decided. High risers. That's where her future was. Way up. She called up Skippy. She called up the bank. They each of them got into their own car and they head for the warehouse. Collateral for a life of investments. The warehouse is laying out there in Jersey, in the sun, beautiful, grass all around, a swamp in the back, barbed wire, electrified in case of trouble, a watchman, the windows clean. The bank takes one look, the warehouse is so stuffed, stovepipes are sticking out the window, cable is rolling off the gutters, the bank doesn't have to look twice. It signs right away on the dotted line.

Oh Anna Marie! Out of her head all that came. Jerry, she asks me, what do you use your head for, headaches? Headaches. How come I'm not one of them, Kitty? I asked Skippy for a house once. He said, Sure, I'll give a $35,000 house for maybe 22. Is that good, Kitty? Should he have given it to me straight, Kitty? Oh, if I could lay my hand on some of that jack, if you figure me out a way.

I wish I could help you be more crooked, said Kitty.

He put his hand on Kitty's high belly. Kitty, I would personally put that kid in Harvard if I could figure the right angle.

Well, what happened to Zandakis?

What'd you bring him up for? He's no businessman, he's a murderer and a creep.

Where's Gladstein?

Him too? He doesn't exist. They hung him up by his thumbs in his five-and-ten on 125th Street with mercerized cotton no. 9.

God?

Kitty, you're laughing at me. Don't laugh.

O.K., said Kitty and leaned back into the deep pillows. She thought life on Sunday was worth two weeks of waiting.

Now me, said Jerry. What I am really: I am the Sunday-breakfast chef. I will make thirty pancakes, six per person, eggs, bacon, fresh ham and a gallon of juice. I will wake up those lazy kids of yours, and I will feed them and feed them until I see some brains wiggling in their dumb heads. I hate a dumb kid. I always think it's me.

Oh, Jerry, said Kitty, what would I do without you?

Well, you wouldn't be knocked up is one thing, he said.

Is that so? said Kitty.

It wasn't cold, but she snuggled down deep under the blanket. It was her friend Faith's grandmother's patchwork quilt that kept her so warm in the warm room. The old windowshades made the morning dusk. She listened to the song of Jerry's brother Skippy's orange radio which was:

"Come, come, ye sons of art . . ."

The bacon curled fearfully on the hot griddle, the waffles popped out of the toaster, and a countertenor called:

> Strike the viol
> Touch
>     oh touch the lute . . .

Well, it was on account of the queen's birthday, the radio commentator said, that such a lot of joy had been transacted in England the busy country, one day when Purcell lived.

# Faith
in
a
Tree

Just when I most needed important conversation, a sniff of the man-wide world, that is, at least one brainy companion who could translate my friendly language into his tongue of undying carnal love, I was forced to lounge in our neighborhood park, surrounded by children.

All the children were there. Among the trees, in the arms of statues, toes in the grass, they hopped in and out of dog shit and dug tunnels into mole holes. Wherever the children ran, their mothers stopped to talk.

What a place in democratic time! One God, who was King of the Jews, who unravels the stars to this day with little hydrogen explosions, He can look down from His Holy Headquarters and see us all: heads of girl, ponytails riding the springtime luck, short black bobs, and an occasional eminence of golden wedding rings. He sees south into Brooklyn how Prospect Park lies in its sand-rooted trees among Japanese gardens and police, and beyond us north to dangerous Central Park. Far north, the deer-eyed eland and kudu survive, grazing the open pits of the Bronx Zoo.

But me, the creation of His soft second thought, I am sitting on the twelve-foot-high, strong, long arm of a sycamore, my feet swinging, and I can only see Kitty, a co-worker in the mother trade—a topnotch crafts-

man. She is below, leaning on my tree, rumpled in a
black cotton skirt made of shroud remnants at about
fourteen cents a yard. Another colleague, Anne Kraat,
is close by on a hard park bench, gloomy, beautiful,
waiting for her luck to change.

Although I can't see them, I know that on the other
side of the dry pool, the thick snout of the fountain
spout, hurrying along the circumference of the parched
sun-struck circle (in which, when Henry James could
see, he saw lilies floating), Mrs. Hyme Caraway pokes
her terrible seedlings, Gowan, Michael, and Christo-
pher, astride an English bike, a French tricycle, and a
Danish tractor. Beside her, talking all the time in fear
of no response, Mrs. Steamy Lewis, mother of Mat-
thew, Mark, and Lucy, tells of happy happy life in a
thatched hotel on a Greek island where total historical
recall is indigenous. Lucy limps along at her skirt in
muddy cashmere. Mrs. Steamy Lewis really swings within the seconds of her latitude and swears she will have
six, but Mr. Steamy Lewis is not expected to live.

I can easily see Mrs. Junius Finn, my up-the-block
neighbor and evening stoop companion, a broad barge,
like a lady, moving slow—a couple of redheaded ca-
booses dragged by clothesline at her stern; on her fat
upper deck, Wiltwyck,* a pale three-year-old roaring
captain with smoky eyes, shoves his wet thumb into
the wind. "Hurry! Hurry!" he howls. Mrs. Finn goes
puff puffing toward the opinionated playground, that
sandy harbor.

Along the same channel, but near enough now to
spatter with spite, tilting delicately like a boy's sailboat, Lynn Ballard floats past my unconcern to drop

---

*Wiltwyck is named for the school of his brother Junior, where
Junior, who was bad and getting worse, is still bad, but is
getting better (as man *is* perfectible).

light anchor, a large mauve handbag, over the green bench slats. She sighs and looks up to see what (if anything) the heavens are telling. In this way, once a week, toes in, head high and in three-quarter turn, arms at her side, graceful as a seal's flippers, she rests, quiet and expensive. She never grabs another mother's kid when he falls and cries. Her particular Michael on his little red bike rides round and round the sandbox, while she dreams of private midnight.

"Like a model," hollers Mrs. Junius Finn over Lynn Ballard's head.

I'm too close to the subject to remark. I sniff, however, and accidentally take sweetness into my lungs. Because it's the month of May.

Kitty and I are nothing like Lynn Ballard. You will see Kitty's darling face, as I tell her, slowly, but me—quick—what am I? Not bad if you're a basement shopper. On my face are a dozen messages, easy to read, strictly for friends, Bargains Galore! I admit it now.

However, the most ordinary life is illuminated by a great event like fame. Once I was famous. From the meaning of that glow, the modest hardhearted me is descended.

Once, all the New York papers that had the machinery to do so carried a rotogravure picture of me in a stewardess's arms. I was, it is now thought, the third commercial air-flight baby passenger in the entire world. This picture is at the Home now, mounted on laundry cardboard. My mother fixed it with glass to assail eternity. The caption says: One of Our Youngest. Little Faith Decided to Visit Gramma. Here She Is, Gently Cuddled in the Arms of Stewardess Jeannie Carter.

*Why* would anyone send a little baby anywhere

alone? What was my mother trying to prove? That I
was independent? That she wasn't the sort to hang on?
That in the sensible, socialist, Zionist world of the future, she wouldn't cry at my wedding? "You're an
American child. Free. Independent." Now what does
that mean? I have always required a man to be de-
pendent on, even when it appeared that I had one
already. I own two small boys whose dependence on
me takes up my lumpen time and my bourgeois feelings. I'm not the least bit ashamed to say that I tie
their shoes and I have wiped their backsides well beyond the recommendations of my friends, Ellen and
George Hellesbraun, who are psychiatric social work-
ers and appalled. I kiss those kids forty times a day. I
punch them just like a father would. When I have a
date and come home late at night, I wake them with a
couple of good hard shakes to complain about the
miserable entertainment. When I'm not furiously exhausted from my low-level job and that bedraggled
soot-slimy house, I praise God for them. One Sunday
morning, my neighbor, Mrs. Raftery, called the cops
because it was 3 a.m. and I was vengefully singing a
praising song.

Since I have already mentioned singing, I have to
tell you: it is not Sunday. For that reason, all the blue-
eyed, boy-faced policemen in the park are worried.
They can see that lots of our vitamin-enlarged high-
school kids are planning to lug their guitar cases
around all day long. They're scared that one of them
may strum and sing a mountain melody or that several,
a gang, will gather to raise their voices in medieval
counterpoint.

Question: Does the world know, does the average
freedman realize that, except for a few hours on Sunday afternoon, the playing of fretted instruments is

banned by municipal decree? Absolutely forbidden is the song of the flute and oboe.

Answer (explanation): This *is* a great ballswinger of a city on the constant cement-mixing remake, battering and shattering, and a high note out of a wild clarinet could be the decibel to break a citizen's eardrum. But what if you were a city-loving planner leaning on your drawing board? Tears would drop to the delicate drafting sheets.

Well, you won't be pulled in for whistling and here come the whistlers—the young Saturday fathers, open-shirted and ambitious. By and large they are trying to get somewhere and have to go to a lot of parties. They are sleepy but pretend to great energy for the sake of their two-year-old sons (little boys need a recollection of Energy as a male resource). They carry miniature footballs though the season's changing. Then the older fathers trot in, just a few minutes slower, their faces scraped to a clean smile, every one of them wearing a fine gray head and eager eyes, his breath caught, his hand held by the baby daughter of a third intelligent marriage.

One of them, passing my tree, stubs his toe on Kitty's sandal. He shades his eyes to look up at me against my sun. That is Alex O. Steele, who was a man organizing tenant strikes on Ocean Parkway when I was a Coney Island Girl Scout against my mother's socialist will. He says, "Hey, Faith, how's the world? Heard anything from Ricardo?"

I answer him in lecture form:

Alex Steele. Sasha. Yes. I have heard from Ricardo. Ricardo even at the present moment when I am trying to talk with you in a civilized way, Ricardo has rolled his dove-gray brain into a glob of spit in order to fly secretly into my ear right off the poop deck of Foamline's World Tour Cruiseship *Eastern Sunset*. He is stretched out in my head, exhausted before dawn from falling in love with an *Eastern Sunset* lady passenger on the first leg of her many-masted journey round the nighttimes of the world. He is *this minute* saying to me,

"Arcturus Rise, Orion Fall . . ."

"Cock-proud son of a bitch," I mutter.

"Ugh," he says, blinking.

"How are the boys?" I make him say.

"Well, he really wants to know how the boys are," I reply.

"No, I don't," he says. "Please don't answer. Just make sure they don't get killed crossing the street. That's your job."

"What?" says Alex Steele. "Speak clearly, Faith, you're garbling like you used to."

"I'm joking. Forget it. But I did hear from him the other day." Out of the pocket of my stretch denims I drag a mashed letter with the exotic stamp of a new underdeveloped nation. It is a large stamp with two smiling lions on a field of barbed wire. The letter says: "I am not well. I hope I never see another rain forest. I am sick. Are you working? Have you seen Ed Snead? He owes me $180. Don't badger him about it if he looks broke. Otherwise send me some to Guerra Verde c/o Dotty Wasserman. Am living here with her. She's on a Children's Mission. Wonderful girl. Reminds me of you ten years ago. She acts on her principles. I *need* the money."

"That is Ricardo. Isn't it, Alex? I mean, there's no signature."

"Dotty Wasserman!" Alex says. "So that's where she is . . . a funny plain girl. Faith, let's have lunch some time. I work up in the East Fifties. How're your folks? I hear they put themselves into a Home. They're young for that. Listen, I'm the executive director of Incurables, Inc., a fund-raising organization. We do wonderful things, Faith. The speed of life-extending developments . . . By the way, what do you think of this little curly Sharon of mine?"

"Oh, Alex, how old is she? She's darling, she's a little golden baby, I love her. She's a peach."

"Of course! *She's* a peach, you like anyone better'n you like us," says my son Richard, who is jealous—because he came first and was deprived at two and one half by his baby brother of my singlehearted love, my friend Ellie Hellesbraun says. Of course, that's a convenient professional lie, a cheap hindsight, as Richard, my oldest son, is brilliant, and I knew it from the beginning. When he was a baby all alone with me, and Ricardo his daddy was off exploring some deep creepy jungle, we often took the ferry to Staten Island. Then we sometimes took the ferry to Hoboken. We walked bridges, just he and I, I said to him, Richie, see the choo choos on the barges, Richie, see the strong fast tugboat, see the merchant ships with their tall cranes, see the *United States* sail away for a week and a day, see the Hudson River with its white current. Oh, it isn't really the Hudson River, I told him, it's the North River; it isn't really a river, it's an estuary, part of the sea, I told him, though he was only two. I could tell him scientific things like that, because I considered him absolutely brilliant. See how beautiful the ice is on the river, see the stony palisades, I said, I hugged him, my pussycat, I said, see the interesting world.

So he really has no kicks coming, he's just peevish.

"We're really a problem to you, Faith, we keep you not free," Richard says. "Anyway, it's true you're crazy about anyone but us."

It's true I do like the other kids. I am not too cool to say Alex's Sharon really is a peach. But you, you stupid kid, Richard! Who could match me for pride or you for brilliance? Which one of the smart third-grade kids in a class of learned Jews, Presbyterians, and bohemians? You are one of the two smartest and the other one is Chinese—Arnold Lee, who does make Richard look a little simple, I admit it. But did you ever hear of a child who, when asked to write a sentence for the word "who" (they were up to the hard *wh*'s), wrote and then magnificently, with Oriental lisp, read the following: "Friend, tell me WHO among the Shanghai merchants does the largest trade?" *

"That's a typical yak yak out of you, Faith," says Richard.

"Now Richard, listen to me, Arnold's an interesting boy; you wouldn't meet a kid like him anywhere but here or Hong Kong. So use some of these advantages I've given you. I could be living in the country, which I love, but I know how hard that is on children—I stay here in this creepy slum. I dwell in soot and slime just so you can meet kids like Arnold Lee and live on this wonderful block with all the Irish and Puerto Ricans, although God knows why there aren't any Negro children for you to play with . . ."

"Who needs it?" he says, just to tease me. "All those guys got knives anyway. But you don't care if I get killed much, do you?"

How can you answer that boy?

*The teacher, Marilyn Gewirtz, the only real person in this story, a child admirer, told me this.

"You don't," says Mrs. Junius Finn, glad to say a few words. "You don't have to answer them. God didn't give out tongues for that. You answer too much, Faith Asbury, and it shows. Nobody fresher than Richard."

"Mrs. Finn," I scream in order to be heard, for she's some distance away and doesn't pay attention the way I do, "what's so terrible about fresh. EVIL is bad. WICKED is bad. ROBBING, MURDER, and PUTTING HEROIN IN YOUR BLOOD is bad."

"Blah blah," she says, deaf to passion. "Blah to you."

Despite no education, Mrs. Finn always is more in charge of word meanings than I am. She is especially in charge of Good and Bad. My language limitations here are real. My vocabulary is adequate for writing notes and keeping journals but absolutely useless for an active moral life. If I really knew this language, there would surely be in my head, as there is in Webster's or the *Dictionary of American Slang*, that unreducible verb designed to tell a person like me what to do next.

Mrs. Finn knows my problems because I do not keep them to myself. And I am reminded of them particularly at this moment, for I see her roughly the size of life, held up at the playground by Wyllie, who has rolled off the high ruddy deck of her chest to admire all the English bikes filed in the park bike stand. Of course that is what Junior is upstate for: love that forced possession. At first his father laced him on his behind, cutting the exquisite design known to generations of daddies who labored at home before the rise of industrialism and group therapy. Then Mr. Finn remembered his childhood, that it was Adam's Fall not Junior that was responsible. Now the Finns never see a ten-speed Italian racer without family sighs for Junior, who is still not home as there were about 176 bikes he loved.

Something is wrong with the following tenants: Mrs. Finn, Mrs. Raftery, Ginnie, and me. Everyone else in our building is on the way up through the affluent society, putting five to ten years into low rent before moving to Jersey or Bridgeport. But our four family units, as people are now called, are doomed to stand culturally still as this society moves on its caterpillar treads from ordinary affluent to absolute empire. All this in mind, I name names and dates. "Mrs. Finn, darling, look at my Richard, the time Junior took his Schwinn and how Richard hid in the coal in the basement thinking of a way to commit suicide," but she coolly answers, "Faith, you're not a bit fair, for Junior give it right back when he found out it was Richard's."

O.K.

Kitty says, "Faith, you'll fall out of the tree, calm yourself." She looks up, rolling her eyes to show direction, and I see a handsome man in narrow pants whom we remember from other Saturdays. He has gone to sit beside Lynn Ballard. He speaks softly to her left ear while she maintains her profile. He has never spoken to her Michael. He is a famous actor trying to persuade her to play opposite him in a new production of *She*. That's what Kitty, my kind friend, says.

I am above that kindness. I often see through the appearance of things right to the apparition itself. It's obvious that he's a weekend queer, talking her into the possibilities of a neighborhood threesome. When her nose quivers and she agrees, he will easily get his really true love, the magnificent manager of the supermarket, who has been longing for her at the check-out counter. What they will do then, I haven't the vaguest idea. I am the child of puritans and I'm only halfway here.

"Don't even think like that," says Kitty. No. She can see a contract in his pocket.

There is no one like Kitty Skazka. Unlike other people who have similar flaws that doom, she is tolerant and loving. I wish Kitty could live forever, bearing daughters and sons to open the heart of man. Meanwhile, mortal, pregnant, she has three green-eyed daughters and they aren't that great. Of course, Kitty thinks they are. And they are no worse than the average gifted, sensitive child of a wholehearted mother and half-a-dozen transient fathers.

Her youngest girl is Antonia, who has no respect for grownups. Kitty has always liked her to have no respect; so in this, she is quite satisfactory to Kitty.

At some right moment on this Saturday afternoon, Antonia decided to talk to Tonto, my second son. He lay on his belly in the grass, his bare heels exposed to the eye of flitting angels, and he worked at a game that included certain ants and other bugs as players.

"Tonto," she asked, "what are you playing, can I?"

"No, it's my game, no girls," Tonto said.

"Are you the boss of the world?" Antonia asked politely.

"Yes," said Tonto.

He thinks, he really believes, he is. To which I must say, Righto! you *are* the boss of the world, Anthony, you are prince of the day-care center for the deprived children of working mothers, you are the Lord of the West Side loading zone whenever it rains on Sundays. I have seen you, creepy chief of the dark forest of four ginkgo trees. The Boss! If you would only look up,

Anthony, and boss me what to do, I would immediately slide down this scabby bark, ripping my new stretch slacks, and do it.

"Give me a nickel, Faith," he ordered at once.

"Give him a nickel, Kitty," I said.

"Nickels, nickels, nickels, whatever happened to pennies?" Anna Kraat asked.

"Anna, you're rich. You're against us," I whispered, but loud enough to be heard by Mrs. Junius Finn, still stopped at the mouth of the playground.

"Don't blame the rich for everything," she warned. She herself, despite the personal facts of her economic position, is disgusted with the neurotic rise of the working class.

Lynn Ballard bent her proud and shameless head.

Kitty sighed, shifted her yardage, and began to shorten the hem of the enormous skirt which she was wearing. "Here's a nickel, love," she said.

"Oh boy! Love!" said Anna Kraat.

Antonia walked in a wide circle around the sycamore tree and put her arm on Kitty, who sewed, the sun just barely over her left shoulder—a perfect light. At that very moment, a representational artist passed. I think it was Edward Roster. He stopped and kneeled, peering at the scene. He squared them off with a film-maker's view-finder and said, "Ah, what a picture!" then left.

"Number one!" I announced to Kitty, which he was, the very first of the squint-eyed speculators who come by to size up the stock. Pretty soon, depending on age and intention, they would move in groups along the paths or separately take notes in the shadows of the statues.

"The trick," said Anna, downgrading the world, "is to know the speculators from the investors . . ."

"I will never live like that. Not I," Kitty said softly.

"Balls!" I shouted, as two men strolled past us, leaning toward one another. They were not fairies, they were Jack Resnick and Tom Weed, music lovers inclining toward their transistor, which was playing the "Chromatic Fantasy." They paid no attention to us because of their relation to this great music. However, Anna heard them say, "Jack, do you hear what I hear?" "Dammit yes, the over-romanticizing and the under-Baching, I can't believe it."

Well, I must say when darkness covers the earth and great darkness the people, I will think of you: two men with smart ears. I don't believe civilization can do a lot more than educate a person's senses. If it's truth and honor you want to refine, I think the Jews have some insight. Make no images, imitate no God. After all, in His field, the graphic arts, He is pre-eminent. Then let that One who made the tan deserts and the blue Van Allen belt and the green mountains of New England be in charge of Beauty, which He obviously understands, and let man, who was full of forgiveness at Jerusalem, and full of survival at Troy, let man be in charge of Good.

"Faith, will you quit with your all-the-time philosophies," says Richard, my first- and disapproving-born. Into our midst, he'd galloped, riding an all-day rage. Brand-new ball bearings, roller skates, heavy enough for his big feet, hung round his neck.

I decided not to give into Richard by responding. I digressed and was free: A cross-eyed man with a red beard became president of the Parent-Teachers Association. He appointed a committee of fun-loving ladies who met in the lunchroom and touched up the coffee with little gurgles of brandy.

He had many clever notions about how to deal with

the money shortage in the public schools. One of his great plots was to promote the idea of the integrated school in such a way that private-school people would think their kids were missing the real thing. And at 5 a.m., the envious hour, the very pit of the morning of middle age, they would think of all the public-school children deeply involved in the urban tragedy, something their children might never know. He suggested that one month of public-school attendance might become part of the private-school curriculum, as natural and progressive an experience as a visit to the boiler room in first grade. Funds could be split 50–50 or 30–70 or 40–60 with the Board of Education. If the plan failed, still the projected effort would certainly enhance the prestige of the public school.

Actually something did stir. Delegations of private progressive-school parents attacked the Board of Ed. for what became known as the Shut-out, and finally even the parents-and-teachers associations of the classical schools (whose peculiar concern always had been educating the child's head) began to consider the value of exposing children who had read about the horror at Ilium to ordinary street fights, so they could understand the *Iliad* better. Public School (in Manhattan) would become a minor like typing, required but secondary.

Mr. Terry Koln, full of initiative, energy, and light-heartedness, was re-elected by unanimous vote and sent on to the United Parents and Federated Teachers Organization as special council member, where in a tiny office all his own he grew marijuana on the windowsills, swearing it was deflowered marigolds.

He was the joy of our P.T.A. But it was soon discovered that he had no children, and Kitty and I have to meet him now surreptitiously in bars.

black place, a man, woman, or child who can think up a pastoral reply like that?

For that reason I looked at him. He had dark offended eyes deep in shadow, with a narrow rim of whiteness under the eyes, the result, I invented, of lots of late carousing nights, followed by eye-wrinkling examinations of mortalness. All this had marked him lightly with sobriety, the first enhancing manifest of ravage.

Even Richard is stunned by this uncynical open-hearted notation of feeling. Forty bare seconds then, while Jack Resnick puts his transistor into the hollow of an English elm, takes a tattered score of *The Messiah* out of his rucksack, and writes a short Elizabethan melody in among the long chorus holds to go with the last singing sentence of my ode to Phillip.

"Nice day," said Anna.

"Please, Faith," said Richard. "Please. You see that guy over there?" He pointed to a fat boy seated among adults on a park bench not far from listening Lynn Ballard. "He has a skate key and he won't lend it to me. He stinks. It's your fault you lost the skate key, Faith. You know you did. You never put anything away."

"Ask him again, Richard."

"You ask him, Faith. You're a grownup."

"I will not. You want the skate key, you ask him. You have to go after your own things in this life. I'm not going to be around forever."

Richard gave me a gloomy, lip-curling look. No. It was worse than that. It was a baleful, foreboding look; a look which as far as our far-in-the-future relations were concerned could be named ill-auguring.

"You never do me a favor, do you?" he said.

*"I'll* go with you, Richard." Phillip grabbed his hand. "We'll talk to that kid. He probably hasn't got a friend in the world. I'm not kidding you, boy, it's hard to be a fat kid." He rapped his belly, where, I imagine, certain memories were stored.

Then he took Richard's hand and they went off, man and boy, to tangle.

"Kitty! Richard just hands him his skate, his hand, and just goes off with him . . . That's not like my Richard."

"Children sense how good he is," said Kitty.

"He's good?"

"He's really not *so* good. Oh, he's good. He's considerate. You know what kind he is, Faith. But if you don't really want him to be good, he will be. And he's very strong. Physically. Someday I'll tell you about him. Not now. He has a special meaning to me."

Actually everyone has a special meaning to Kitty, even me, a dictionary of particular generalities, even Anna and all our children.

Kitty sewed as she spoke. She looked like a delegate to a Conference of Youth from the People's Republic of Ubmonsk from Lower Tartaria. A single dark braid hung down her back. She wore a round-necked white blouse with capped sleeves made of softened muslin, woven for aged bridesbeds. I have always listened carefully to my friend Kitty's recommendations, for she has made one mistake after another. Her experience is invaluable.

Kitty's kids have kept an eye on her from their dear tiniest times. They listened to her reasons, but the two eldest, without meaning any disrespect, had made different plans for their lives. Children are all for John Dewey. Lisa and Nina have never believed that Kitty's life really worked. They slapped Antonia for scratching the enameled kitchen table. When Kitty caught them, she said, "Antonia's a baby. Come on now girls, what's a table?"

"What's a *table?*" said Lisa. "What a nut! She wants to know what a table is."

"Well, Faith," said Richard, "*he* got the key for me." Richard and Phillip were holding hands, which made Richard look like a little boy with a daddy. I could cry when I think that I always treat Richard as though he's about forty-seven.

Phillip felt remarkable to have extracted that key. "He's quite a kid, Faith, your boy. I wish that my Johnny in Chicago was as great as Richard here. Is Johnny really nine, Kitty?"

"You bet," she said.

He kept his puzzled face for some anticipated eventuality and folded down to cross-legged comfort, leaning familiarly on Nina and Lisa's backs. "How are you two fairy queens?" he asked and tugged at their long hair gently. He peeked over their shoulders. They were reading Classic Comics, *Ivanhoe* and *Robin Hood*.

"I hate to read," said Antonia.

"Me too," hollered Tonto.

"Antonia, I wish *you'd* read more," said Phillip. "Antonia, little beauty. These two little ones. Forest babies. Little sunny brown creatures. I think *you* would say, Kitty, that they understand their bodies?"

"Oh, yes, I would," said Kitty, who believed all that.

Although I'm very shy, I tend to persevere, so I said, "You're pretty sunny and brown yourself. How do you make out? What are you? An actor or a French teacher, or something?"

"French . . ." Kitty smiled. "He could teach Sanskrit if he wanted to. Or Filipino or Cambodian."

"Cambodge . . ." Phillip said. He said this softly as

though the wars in Indochina might be the next subject for discussion.

"French teacher?" asked Anna Kraat, who had been silent, grieved by spring, for one hour and forty minutes. "Judy," she yelled into the crossed branches of the sycamore. "Judy . . . French . . ."

"So?" said Judy. "What's so great? Je m'appelle Judy Solomon. Ma père s'appelle Pierre Solomon. How's that, folks?"

"Mon père," said Anna. "I told you that before."

"Who cares?" said Judy, who didn't care.

"She's lost two fathers," said Anna, "within three years."

Tonto stood up to scratch his belly and back, which were itchy with wet grass. "Mostly nobody has fathers, Anna," he said.

"Is that true, little boy?" asked Phillip.

"Oh yes," Tonto said. "My father is in the Equator. They never even had fathers," pointing to Kitty's daughters. "Judy has two fathers, Peter and Dr. Kraat. Dr. Kraat takes care of you if you're crazy."

"Maybe I'll be your father."

Tonto looked at me. I was too rosy. "Oh no," he said. "Not right now. My father's name is Ricardo. He's a famous explorer. Like an explorer, I mean. He went in the Equator to make contacts. I have two books by him."

"Do you like him?"

"He's all right."

"Do you miss him?"

"He's very fresh when he's home."

"That's enough of that!" I said. It's stupid to let a kid talk badly about his father in front of another man. Men really have too much on their minds without that.

"He's quite a boy," said Phillip. "You and your

brother are real boys." He turned to me. "What do I
do? Well, I make a living. Here. Chicago. Wherever I
am. I'm not in financial trouble. I figured it all out
ten years ago. But what I really am, really . . ." he
said, driven to lying confidence because he thought he
ought to try that life anyway. "What I truly am is a
comedian."

"That's a joke, that's the first joke you've said."

"But that's what I want to be . . . a comedian."

"But you're not funny."

"But I am. You don't know me yet. I want to be
one. I've been a teacher and I've worked for the State
Department. And now what I want to be's a comedian.
People have changed professions before."

"You can't be a comedian," said Anna, "unless
you're funny."

He took a good look at Anna. Anna's character is
terrible, but she's beautiful. It took her husbands about
two years apiece to see how bad she was, but it takes
the average passer, answerer, or asker about thirty seconds to see how beautiful she is. You can't warn
men. As for Kitty and me, well, we love her because
she's beautiful.

"Anna's all right," said Richard.

"Be quiet," said Phillip. "Say, Anna, are you interested in the French tongue, the French people, French
history, or French civilization?"

"No," said Anna.

"Oh," he said, disappointed.

"I'm not interested in anything," said Anna.

"Say!" said Phillip, getting absolutely red with excitement, blushing from his earlobes down into his
shirt, making me think as I watched the blood descend
from his brains that I would like to be the one who
was holding his balls very gently, to be exactly present

so to speak when all the thumping got there.

Since it was clearly Anna, not I, who would be in that affectionate position, I thought I'd better climb the tree again just for the oxygen or I'd surely suffer the same sudden descent of blood. That's the way nature does things, swishing those quarts and quarts to wherever they're needed for power and action.

Luckily, a banging of pots and pans came out of the playground and a short parade appeared—four or five grownups, a few years behind me in the mommy-and-daddy business, pushing little go-carts with babies in them, a couple of three-year-olds hanging on. They were the main bangers and clangers. The grownups carried three posters. The first showed a prime-living, prime-earning, well-dressed man about thirty-five years old next to a small girl. A question was asked: WOULD YOU BURN A CHILD? In the next poster he placed a burning cigarette on the child's arm. The cool answer was given: WHEN NECESSARY. The third poster carried no words, only a napalmed Vietnamese baby, seared, scarred, with twisted hands.

We were very quiet. Kitty put her head down into the dark skirt of her lap. I trembled. I said, Oh! Anna said to Phillip, "They'll only turn people against them," and turned against them herself at once.

"You people will have to go," said Douglas, our neighborhood cop. He had actually arrived a few minutes earlier to tell Kitty to beg Jerry not to sell grass at this end of the park. But he was ready. "You just have to go," he said. "No parades in the park."

Kitty lifted her head and with sweet bossiness said, "Hey Doug, leave them alone. They're O.K."

Tonto said, "I know that girl, she goes to Greenwich House. You're in the fours," he told her.

Doug said, "Listen Tonto, there's a war on. You'll

be a soldier too someday. I know you're no sissy like
some kids around here. You'll fight for your country."

"Ha ha," said Mrs. Junius Finn, "that'll be the day.
Oh, say, can you see?"

The paraders made a little meeting just outside our
discussion. They had to decide what next. The four
grownups held the tongues of the children's bells until
that decision could be made. They were a group of that
kind of person.

"What they're doing is treason," said Douglas. He
had decided to explain and educate. "Signs on sticks
aren't allowed. In case of riot. It's for their own protection too. They might turn against each other." He
was afraid that no one would find the real perpetrator
if that should happen.

"But Officer, I know these people. They're decent
citizens of this community," said Phillip, though he
didn't live in the borough, city, or state, let alone vote
in it.

Doug looked at him thoroughly. "Mister, I could
take you in for interference." He pulled his cop voice
out of his healthy diaphragm.

"Come on . . ." said Kitty.

"You too," he said fiercely. "Disperse," he said,
"disperse, disperse."

Behind his back, the meeting had been neatly dis-
persed for about three minutes. He ran after them, but
they continued on the park's circumference, their posters on the carriage handles, very solemn, making
friends and enemies.

"They look pretty legal to me," I hollered after
Doug's blue back.

Tonto fastened himself to my leg and stuck his
thumb in his mouth.

Richard shouted, "Ha! Ha!" and punched me. He

also began to grind his teeth, which would lead, I knew, to great expense.

"Oh, that's funny, Faith," he said. He cried, he stamped his feet dangerously, in skates. "I hate you. I hate your stupid friends. Why didn't they just stand up to that stupid cop and say fuck you. They should of just stood up and hit him." He ripped his skates off, twisting his bad ankle. "Gimme that chalk box, Lisa, just give it to me."

In a fury of tears and disgust, he wrote on the near blacktop in pink flamingo chalk—in letters fifteen feet high, so the entire Saturday walking world could see— WOULD YOU BURN A CHILD? and under it, a little taller, the red reply, WHEN NECESSARY.

And I think that is exactly when events turned me around, changing my hairdo, my job uptown, my style of living and telling. Then I met women and men in different lines of work, whose minds were made up and directed out of that sexy playground by my children's heartfelt brains, I thought more and more and every day about the world.

Samuel

Some boys are very tough. They're afraid of nothing. They are the ones who climb a wall and take a bow at the top. Not only are they brave on the roof, but they make a lot of noise in the darkest part of the cellar where even the super hates to go. They also jiggle and hop on the platform between the locked doors of the subway cars.

Four boys are jiggling on the swaying platform. Their names are Alfred, Calvin, Samuel, and Tom. The men and the women in the cars on either side watch them. They don't like them to jiggle or jump but don't want to interfere. Of course some of the men in the cars were once brave boys like these. One of them had ridden the tail of a speeding truck from New York to Rockaway Beach without getting off, without his sore fingers losing hold. Nothing happened to him then or later. He had made a compact with other boys who preferred to watch: Starting at Eighth Avenue and Fifteenth Street, he would get to some specified place, maybe Twenty-third and the river, by hopping the tops of the moving trucks. This was hard to do when one truck turned a corner in the wrong direction and the nearest truck was a couple of feet too high. He made three or four starts before succeeding. He had gotten this idea from a film at school called *The Ro-*

*mance of Logging.* He had finished high school, married a good friend, was in a responsible job and going to night school.

These two men and others looked at the four boys jumping and jiggling on the platform and thought, It must be fun to ride that way, especially now the weather is nice and we're out of the tunnel and way high over the Bronx. Then they thought, These kids do seem to be acting sort of stupid. They *are* little. Then they thought of some of the brave things they had done when they were boys and jiggling didn't seem so risky.

The ladies in the car became very angry when they looked at the four boys. Most of them brought their brows together and hoped the boys could see their extreme disapproval. One of the ladies wanted to get up and say, Be careful you dumb kids, get off that platform or I'll call a cop. But three of the boys were Negroes and the fourth was something else she couldn't tell for sure. She was afraid they'd be fresh and laugh at her and embarrass her. She wasn't afraid they'd hit her, but she was afraid of embarrassment. Another lady thought, Their mothers never know where they are. It wasn't true in this particular case. Their mothers all knew that they had gone to see the missile exhibit on Fourteenth Street.

Out on the platform, whenever the train accelerated, the boys would raise their hands and point them up to the sky to act like rockets going off, then they rat-tat-tatted the shatterproof glass pane like machine guns, although no machine guns had been exhibited.

For some reason known only to the motorman, the train began a sudden slowdown. The lady who was afraid of embarrassment saw the boys jerk forward and backward and grab the swinging guard chains. She had her own boy at home. She stood up with determination and went to the door. She slid it open and said, "You boys will be hurt. You'll be killed. I'm going to call the conductor if you don't just go into the next car and sit down and be quiet."

Two of the boys said, "Yes'm," and acted as though they were about to go. Two of them blinked their eyes a couple of times and pressed their lips together. The train resumed its speed. The door slid shut, parting the lady and the boys. She leaned against the side door because she had to get off at the next stop.

The boys opened their eyes wide at each other and laughed. The lady blushed. The boys looked at her and laughed harder. They began to pound each other's back. Samuel laughed the hardest and pounded Alfred's back until Alfred coughed and the tears came. Alfred held tight to the chain hook. Samuel pounded him even harder when he saw the tears. He said, "Why you bawling? You a baby, huh?" and laughed. One of the men whose boyhood had been more watchful than brave became angry. He stood up straight and looked at the boys for a couple of seconds. Then he walked in a citizenly way to the end of the car, where he pulled the emergency cord. Almost at once, with a terrible hiss, the pressure of air abandoned the brakes and the wheels were caught and held.

People standing in the most secure places fell forward, then backward. Samuel had let go of his hold on the chain so he could pound Tom as well as Alfred. All the passengers in the cars whipped back and forth, but he pitched only forward and fell head first to be crushed and killed between the cars.

The train had stopped hard, halfway into the station, and the conductor called at once for the trainmen who knew about this kind of death and how to take the body from the wheels and brakes. There was silence except for passengers from other cars who asked, What happened! What happened! The ladies waited around wondering if he might be an only child. The men recalled other afternoons with very bad endings. The little boys stayed close to each other, leaning and touching shoulders and arms and legs.

When the policeman knocked at the door and told her about it, Samuel's mother began to scream. She screamed all day and moaned all night, though the doctors tried to quiet her with pills.

Oh, oh, she hopelessly cried. She did not know how she could ever find another boy like that one. However, she was a young woman and she became pregnant. Then for a few months she was hopeful. The child born to her was a boy. They brought him to be seen and nursed. She smiled. But immediately she saw that this baby wasn't Samuel. She and her husband together have had other children, but never again will a boy exactly like Samuel be known.

# The
# Burdened
# Man

The man has the burden of the money. It's needed day after day. More and more of it. For ordinary things and for life. That's why holidays are a hard time for him. Another hard time is the weekend, when he's not making money or furthering himself.

Then he's home and he watches the continuation of his son's life and the continuation of his wife's life. They do not seem to know about the money. They are not stupid, but they leave the hall lights on. They consume electricity. The wife cooks and cooks. She has to make meat. She has to make potatoes and bring orange juice to the table. He is not against being healthy, but rolls baked hot in expensive gas are not necessary. His son makes phone calls. Then his wife makes a phone call. These are immediately clicked into the apparatus of A T & T and added against him by IBM. One day they accidentally buy three newspapers. Another day the boy's out in the yard. He's always careless. Naturally he falls and rips his pants. This expense occurs on a Saturday. On Sunday a neighbor knocks at the door, furious because it's her son's pants that were first borrowed then ripped, and they cost $5.95 and are good narrow-wale corduroy.

When he hears this, the man is beside himself. He does not know where the money is coming from. The

truth is, he makes a very good salary and puts away
five dollars a week for his son's college. He has done
this every week and now has $2,750 in the bank. But
he does not know where the money for *all* of life will
come from. At the door, without a word, he gives the
neighbor six dollars in cash and receives two cents in
change. He looks at the two pennies in his hand. He
feels penniless and thinks he will faint. In order to be
strong, he throws the two pennies at his neighbor, who
screams, then runs. He chases her for two blocks.
Her husband can't come to her rescue because he's on
Sunday duty. Her children are at the movies. When
she reaches the corner mailbox, she leans against it.
She turns in fear and throws the six dollars at him. He
takes the floating bills out of the air. He pitches them
straight from the shoulder with all his strength. They
drift like leaves to her coat and she cries out, "Stop!
stop!"

The police arrive at once from somewhere and are
disgusted to see two grown-up people throwing money
at each other and crying. But the neighborhood is full
of shade trees and pretty lawns. The police forgive
them and watch them go home in the same direction
(because they're next-door neighbors).

They are sorry for each other's anger.

She says: "I don't need the pants. Billy has plenty of
pants." He says: "What's the money to me? Six dollars? Chicken feed."

Then they have coffee at her house and explain everything. They each tell one story about when they
were young. After this they become friends and visit
one another on Sunday afternoons when both their
families are on duty or at the movies.

On Friday nights the man climbs the three flights out
of the deep subway. He stops at a bakery just before

the bus for his remote neighborhood picks him up. He brings a strawberry shortcake home to his wife and son.

All the same, things changed. Summer came and the neighbor took her three children to a little summer house on the Long Island water. When she returned, she was tanned a light tea color with a touch of orange because of the lotion she had used. It seemed to him that her first and subsequent greetings were very cool. He had answered her cordially. "You look real great," he said. "Thank you," she said, without mentioning his looks, which the vacation sun had also improved.

One Saturday morning he waited in bed for the house to become quiet and empty. His wife and the boy always went to the supermarket by 9 a.m. When they were finally gone with the cart, the shopping bags, and the car, he began to think that he and his neighbor had talked and talked through many Sundays and now it was time to consider different ways to begin to make love to her.

He wondered if the kitchen might not be the best place to start because it was narrow. She was a decent person with three children and would probably say no just to continue her decency a little longer. She would surely try to get away from his first effort. However, she would never get away if he approached at the dishwashing machine.

Another possibility: If the coffee were already on the table, he might be beside her as she prepared to pour. He would take the coffee pot away from her and put it on the trivet. He would then take her hands and look into her eyes. She would know his meaning at once and start all the arrangements in her mind about ensuring privacy for the next Sunday.

Another possibility: In the living room on the

couch before the coffee table, he would straightfor-
wardly yet shyly declare, "I'm having a terrible time.
I want to get together with you." This was the strongest
plan because it required no further plan. He would be
able to embrace her right after making his statement;
he would lift her skirt, and if she wore no girdle, he
could enter her at once.

The next day was Sunday. He called and she said in
her new cool way, "Oh sure, come on over." In about
ten minutes he was waiting for coffee at her dinette
table. He had clipped the first four flowering zinnias
out of his wife's lawn border and was arranging them
in the bowl when he became aware of his neighbor's
husband creeping stealthily along the wall toward him.
He looked foolish and probably drunk. The man said,
"What . . . what . . ." He knew the husband by appearance only and was embarrassed to see him nearly on
his knees in his own house.

"You fucking wop . . ." said the husband. "You
ain't been here twenty minutes you finished already,
you cheap quickie cuntsucker . . . in and out . . . that's
what she likes, the cold bitch . . ."

"No . . . no . . ." said the man. He was saying "No
no," to the husband's belief that she was cold. "No no,"
he said, although he didn't know for sure, "she's not."

"What you waste your time on that fat bag of
tits . . ." said her husband. "Hey!" said the man. He
hadn't thought of that part of her much at all. Mostly
he had thought of how she would be under her skirt
and of her thighs. He realized the husband was drunk
or he would not speak of his wife with such words.

The husband then waved a pistol at him in a drunk-
en way the man had often seen in the movies but never
in life. He knew it was all right for the husband to
have that pistol because he was a cop.

As a cop he was not unknown. He had once killed a farm boy made crazy by crowds in the city. The boy had run all day in terror round and round Central Park. People thought he was a runner because he wore an undershirt, but he had finally entered the park, and with a kitchen knife he had killed one baby and wounded two or three others. "Too many people," he screamed when he killed.

Bravely the cop had disarmed him, but the poor boy pulled another long knife out of his pants-leg pocket and the cop had then had to kill him. He was given a medal for this. He often remembered that afternoon and wondered that he had been brave once, but was not brave enough to have been brave twice.

Now he stared at the man and he tried to remember what inhibition had abandoned him, what fear of his victim had given him energy. How had he decided to kill that crazy boy?

Suddenly the woman came out of the kitchen. She saw that her husband was drunk and bloody-eyed. She saw that he held a pistol and waved it before his eyes as though it could clear fogs and smogs. She remembered that he was a person who had killed.

"Don't touch him," she screamed at her husband. "You maniac! Boy-killer! Don't touch him," she shouted and gathered the man against her whole soft body. He hadn't wanted anything like this, his chin caught in the V neck of her wrap-around housedress.

"Just get out of her shirt," said the husband.

"If you kill him, you kill me," she said, hugging the man so hard he wondered where to turn his nose to get air.

"O.K., why not, why not!" said the husband. "Why not, you fucking whore, why not?"

Then his finger pressed the trigger and he shot and

shot, the man, the woman, the wall, the picture window,
the coffee pot. Looking down, screaming, Whore!
whore! he shot straight into the floor, right through his
shoe, smashing his toes for life.

The midnight edition of the morning paper said:

## QUEENS COP COOLS ROMANCE

*Precinct Pals Clap Cop in Cooler*
Sgt. Armand Kielly put an end today to his wife's
alleged romance with neighbor Alfred Ciaro by
shooting up his kitchen, Mrs. Kielly, himself, and
his career. Arrested by his own pals from the
115th precinct who claim he has been nervous of
late, he faces departmental action. When questioned by this reporter, Mrs. Kielly said, "No no
no."

The burdened man spent three days in the hospital
having his shoulder wound attended to. Hospitalization
paid for nearly all. He then sold his house and moved
to another neighborhood on another bus line, though
the subway stop remained the same.

Until old age startled him, he was hardly unhappy
again.

In fact, for several years, he could really feel each
morning that a mixture of warm refreshments was being
pumped out of the chambers of his heart to all his cold
extremities.

# Enormous
# Changes
# at the
# Last Minute

A young man said he wanted to go to bed with Alexandra because she had an interesting mind. He was a cabdriver and she *had* admired the curly back of his head. Still, she was surprised. He said he would pick her up again in about an hour and a half. Because she was fair and a responsible person, she placed between them a barrier of truthful information. She said, I suppose you don't know many middle-aged women.

You don't look so middle-aged to me. I mean, everyone likes what they like. That is, I'm interested in your point of view, your way of life. Anyway, he said, peering into the mirror, your face is nice and your eyebrows are out of sight.

Make it two hours, she said. I'm visiting my father whom I happen to love.

I love mine too, he said. He just doesn't love me. Too too bad.

O.K. That's enough, she said. Because they had already *had* the following factual and introductory conversation.

How old are your kids?

I have none.

Sorry. Then what do you do for a living?

Children. Early teenage. Adoptions, foster homes. Probation. Troubles—well . . .

Where'd you go to school?

City colleges. What about you?

Oh, me. Lots of places. Antioch. Wisconsin. California. I might go back someday. Some place else though. Maybe Harvard. Why not?

He leaned on his horn to move a sixteen-wheel trailer truck delivering Kleenex to the A & P.

I wish you'd stop that, she said. I hate that kind of driving.

Why? Oh! You're an idealist! He looked through his rearview mirror straight into her eyes. But were you married? Ever?

Once. For years.

Who to?

It's hard to describe. A revolutionist.

Really? Could I know him? What's his name? We say revolutionary nowadays.

Oh?

By the way, my name's Dennis. I probably like you, he said.

You do, do you? Well, why should you? And let me ask you something. What do you mean by nowadays?

By the birdseed of St. Francis, he said, taking a tiny brogue to the tip of his tongue. I meant no harm.

Nowadays! she said. What does that mean? I guess you think you're kind of brand-new. You're not so brand-new. The telephone was brand-new. The airplane was brand-new. *You've* been seen on earth before.

Wow! he said. He stopped the cab just short of the hospital entrance. He turned to look at her and make decisions. But you're right, he said sweetly. You know the mind *is* an astonishing, long-living, erotic thing.

Is it? she asked. Then she wondered: What is the life expectancy of the mind?

the beginning of many twigs. 4. He could talk to her
out the kids, help her to understand their hangups,
ir incredible virtues. He had missed being one of
m by about seven useless years.

o many reasons are not essential, Alexandra said.
offered him a brandy. Holy toads! he said furiously.
know I'm not into that. Touched by gloom, he
n to remove the heavy shoes he wore for mountain
ing. He dropped his pants and stamped on them
uple of times to make sure he and they were dis-
ged.

exandra, in the first summer dress of spring, stood
nd watched. She breathed deeply because of hav-
en alone for a year or two. She put her two hands
er ribs to hold her heart in place and also out of
ty to quiet its immodest thud. Then they went to
the bedroom and made love until that noisy dis-
ce ended. She couldn't hear one interior sound.
ore they slept.

e morning she became interested in reality again,
she had always liked. She wanted to talk about
began with a description of John, her father's
r in the hospital.

s? Far out! Well he's right. And another thing.
is coming. It's coming to the Forest Hills
Fair, the Rikers Island Jamboree, the Fillmore
d the Ecolocountry Gardens in Westchester.
st.

y? A lesson in reality? Am I a cabdriver? No. I
ab but I am not a cabdriver. I'm a song hawk.
aker. I'm a poet, in other words. Do you know
black man walking down the street today is
ut only one white honky devil in ten. One in

\* \* \*

Eighty years, said her father, glad to be useful. Once
he had explained electrical storms before you could
find the Book of Knowledge. Now in the cave of old
age, he continued to amass wonderful information. But
he was sick with oldness. His arteries had a hopeless
future, and conversation about all that obsolescent
tubing often displaced very interesting subjects.

One day he said, Alexandra! Don't show me the sunset again. I'm not interested any more. You know that.
She had just pointed to a simple sunset happening outside his hospital window. It was a red ball—all alone,
without its evening streaking clouds—a red ball falling
hopelessly west, just missing the Hudson River, Jersey
City, Chicago, the Great Plains, the Golden Gate—
falling, falling.

Then in Russian he sighed some Pushkin. Not for
me, the spring. *Nye dyla menya* . . . He slept. She read
the large-print edition of *The Guns of August.* A half
hour later, he opened his eyes and told her how, in that
morning's *Times,* the Phoenicians had sailed to Brazil
in about 500 B.C. A remarkable people. The Vikings
too were remarkable. He spoke well of the Chinese, the
Jews, the Greeks, the Indians—all the old commercial
people. Actually he had never knocked an entire nation. International generosity had been started in him
during the late nineteenth century by his young mother
and father, candleholders inside the dark tyranny of
the czars. It was childhood training. Thoughtfully, he
passed it on.

In the hospital bed next to him, a sufferer named
John feared the imminent rise of the blacks of South
Africa, the desperate blacks of Chicago, the yellow
Chinese, and the Ottoman Turks. He had more reason

than Alexandra's father to dread the future because his heart was strong. He would probably live to see it all. He believed the Turks when they came would bring to New York City diseases like cholera, virulent scarlet fever, and particularly leprosy.

Leprosy! for God's sakes! said Alexandra. John! Upset yourself with reality for once! She read aloud from the *Times* about the bombed, burned lepers' colonies in North Vietnam. Her father said, Please, Alexandra, today, no propaganda. Why do you constantly pick on the United States? He remembered the first time he'd seen the American flag on wild Ellis Island. Under its protection and working like a horse, he'd read Dickens, gone to medical school, and shot like a surface-to-air missile right into the middle class.

Then he said, But they shouldn't put a flag in the middle of the chocolate pudding. It's ridiculous.

It's Memorial Day, said the nurse's aide, removing his tray.

In the early evening Dennis stood at the door of each room of Alexandra's apartment. He looked this way and that. Underuse in a time of population stress, he muttered. He entered the kitchen and sniffed the kitchen air. It doesn't matter, he said aloud. He took a fingerful of gravy out of the pot on the stove. Beef stew, he whispered. Then he opened the door to the freezer compartment and said, Sweet Jesus! because there were eleven batches of the same, neatly stacked and frozen. They were for Alexandra's junkies, whose methadone required lots of protein and carbohydrates.

I wouldn't have them in my house. It's a wonder you got a cup and saucer left. Creeps, said Dennis. However, yes indeed, I will eat this stuff. Why? Does it

make me think of home or of something el; I think, a movie I once saw.

Apple turnovers! You know I have to commune isn't working too well. Probab in Brooklyn and the food coop isn't to; cool, they've accepted the criticism.

You have lots of junk in here, he p dinner. He had decided to give the plac ful attention. He meant armchairs, la her grandmother's wedding portrait, stand with two of her father's canes.

Um, said Alexandra, it's rent-cont

You know what I like to do, Alexa with a girl and look at a late movie, perience common to Americans at th tant to be like others, to dig the aver to be him. Be HIM. It's groovier t gab. You'd be surprised how friend

I'm not against friendliness, she against Americans.

They watched half of *A Day* very relaxing, he said. It's kind o Then he began to undress. He said, Alexandra I really can't wa rise person. I like to go to bed days?

He gave reasons: 1. It was end, and the house in Brooklyn tors. 2. He was disgusted wi they'd given up the most k fashionable tie-dying. 3. He some good walks in the mor to walk in were the lightest the tree on the corner thoug

Nowadays I write for the Lepers all the time. Fuck poetry. The Lepers dig me. I dig them.

The Lepers? Alexandra said.

Cool! You know them? No? Well, you may have known them under their old name. They used to be called The Split Atom. But they became too popular and their thing is anonymity. That's what they're known for. They'll probably change their name after the summer festivals. They might move to the country and call themselves Winter Moss.

Do you really make a living now?

Oh yes. I do. I do. Among technicians like myself I do.

Now: I financially carry one third of a twelve-person, three-children commune. I only drive a cab to keep on top of the world of illusion, you know, Alexandra, to rap with the bourgeoisies, the fancy whores, the straight ladies visiting their daddies. Oh, excuse me, he said.

Now, Alexandra, imagine this: two bass guitars, a country violin, one piccolo, and drums. The Lepers' theme song! He sat up in bed. The sun shone on his chest. He had begun to think of breakfast, but he sang so that Alexandra could know him better and dig his substantialness.

oooooh
first my finger goes     goes     goes
then my nose
        then baby     my toes

if you love me this way     anyway     any day
I'll go your way
        my Little Neck rose

Well? he asked. He looked at Alexandra. Was she

going to cry? I thought you were such a reality freak, Alexandra. That's the way it is in the real world. Anyway! He then said a small prose essay to explain and buttress the poem:

> The kids! the kids! Though terrible troubles hang over them, such as the absolute end of the known world quickly by detonation or slowly through the easygoing destruction of natural resources, they are still, even now, optimistic, humorous, and brave. In fact, they intend enormous changes at the last minute.

Come on, said Alexandra, hardhearted, an enemy of generalization, there are all kinds. My boys aren't like that.

Yes, they are, he said, angry. You bring them around. I'll prove it. Anyway, I love them. He tried for about twenty minutes, forgetting breakfast, to show Alexandra how to look at things in this powerful last-half-of-the-century way. She tried. She had always had a progressive if sometimes reformist disposition, but at that moment, listening to him talk, she could see straight ahead over the thick hot rod of love to solitary age and lonesome death.

But there's nothing to fear my dear girl, her father said. When you get there you will not want to live a hell of a lot. Nothing to fear at all. You will be used up. You are like a coal burning, smoldering. Then there's nothing left to burn. Finished. Believe me, he said, although he hadn't been there yet himself, at that moment you won't mind. Alexandra's face was a bit rumpled, listening.

Don't look at me like that! he said. He was too sensitive to her appearance. He hated her to begin to look older the way she'd had to in the last twenty years. He said, Now *I* have seen people die. A large number. Not one or two. Many. They are good and ready. Pain. Despair. Unconsciousness, nightmares. Perfectly good comas, wrecked by nightmares. They are ready. You will be too, Sashka. Don't worry so much.

Ho ho ho, said John in the next bed listening through the curtains. Doc, I'm not ready. I feel terrible, I got lousy nightmares. I don't sleep a wink. But I'm not ready. I can't piss without this tube. Lonesomeness! Boy! Did you ever see *one* of my kids visiting? No! Still I am *not* ready. N O T   R E A D Y. He spelled it out, looking at the ceiling or through it, to the roof garden for incurables, and from there to God.

The next morning Dennis said, I would rather die than go to the hospital.

For God's sakes why?

Why? Because I hate to be in the hands of strangers. They don't let you take the pills you got that you know work, then if you need one of their pills, even if you buzz, they don't come. The nurse and three interns are making out in the information booth. I've seen it. It's a high counter, she's answering questions, and they're taking turns banging her from behind.

Dennis! You're too dumb. You sound like some superstitious old lady with rape dreams.

That's cool, he said. I *am* an old lady about my health. I mean I like it. I want my teeth to go right on. Right on sister. He began to sing, then stopped. Listen! Your destiny's in their hands. It's up to them. Do you live? Or are you a hippie crawling creep from their point of view? Then die!

Really. Nobody ever decides to let you die. In fact,

that's what's wrong. They decide to keep people alive
for years after death has set in.

You mean like your father?

Alexandra leaped out of bed stark naked. My father! Why he's got twenty times your zip.

Cool it! he said. Come back. I was just starting to
fuck you and you get so freaked.

And another thing. Don't use that word. I hate it.
When you're with a woman you have to use the language that's right for her.

What do you want me to say?

I want you to say, I was just starting to make love
to you, etc.

Well, that's true, said Dennis, I was. When she returned to him, he only touched the tips of her fingers,
though all of her was present. He kissed each finger
and said right after each kiss, I want to make love to
you. He did this sweetly, not sarcastically.

Dennis, Alexandra said in an embarrassment of
recognition, you look like one of my placements, in fact
you look like a kid, Billy Platoon. His real name is
Platon but he calls himself Platoon so he can go to
Vietnam and get killed like his stepbrother. He's a
dreamy boy.

Alexandra, you talk a lot, now hush, no politics.

Alexandra continued for a sentence or two. He car-
ries a stick with a ball full of nails attached, like some
medieval weapon, in case an enemy from Suffolk Street
CIA's him. That's what they call it.

Never heard that before. Besides I'm jealous. And
also I'm the enemy from Suffolk Street.

No, no, said Alexandra. Then she noticed in her
mother's bedroom bureau mirror across the room a
small piece of her naked self. She said, Ugh!

There, there! said Dennis lovingly, caressing what he thought she'd looked at, a couple of rippled inches between her breast and belly. It's natural, Alexandra. Men don't change as much as women. Among all the animals, human females are the only ones to lose estrogen as they get older.

Is that it? she said.

Then there was nothing to talk about for half an hour.

But how come you knew that? she asked. The things you know, Dennis. What for?

Why—for my art, he said. And despite his youth he rested from love the way artists often do in order to sing. He sang:

> Camp out
>      out in the forest daisy
>      under the gallows tree
> with the
>              ace of pentacles
>              and me
>
>
>                      daisy flower
>
> What of the
>              earth's ecology
> you're drivin too fast
> Daisy you're drivin alone
>      Hey Daisy      cut the ignition
>                      let the oil
>                      back in the stone.

Oh, I like that one. I admire it! Alexandra said. But in fact, *is* ecology a good word for a song? It's technical . . .

Any word is good, it's the big word today anyway, said Dennis. It's what you do with the word. The language and the idea, they work it out together.

Really? Where do you get most of your ideas?

I don't know if I want to eat or sleep, he said. I think I just want to nuzzle your titty. Talk talk talk. Most? Well, I would say the majority are from a magazine, the *Scientific American*.

During breakfast, language remained on his mind. Because of this, he was silent. After the pancakes, he said, Actually Alexandra, I *can* use any words I want. And I have. I proved it last week in a conversation just like this one. I asked these blue-eyed cats to give me a dictionary. I just flipped the pages and jabbed and the word I hit was *ophidious*. But I did it, because the word does the dreaming for you. The WORD.

To a tune that was probably "On Top of Old Smoky" he sang:

> The ophidious garden
> was invented by Freud
>
>> where three ladies murdered
>> oh three ladies murdered
>
> the pricks of the birds
>
> the cobra is buried
> the rattlesnake writhes
>
>> in the black snaky garden
>> in the blue snaky garden
>
> in the hairs of my wives.

More coffee, please, he said with pride and modesty.

It's better than most of your songs, Alexandra said.

It's a poem, isn't it? It *is* better.

What? What? It is *not* better, it is not, goddamn. It is not . . . It just isn't . . . oh, excuse me for losing my cool like that.

Forget it sonny, Alexandra said respectfully. I only meant I liked it, but I know, I'm too frank from living alone so much I think. Anyway, how come you always think about wives? Wives, mothers?

Because that's me, said peaceful Dennis. Haven't you noticed it yet? That's my bag. I'm a motherfucker.

Oh, she said, I see. But I'm not a mother, Dennis.

Yes, you are, Alexandra. I've figured out a lot about you. I know. I act like the weekend stud sometimes. But I wrote you a song. Just last night in the cab. I think about you. The Lepers'll never dig it. They don't know too much about life. They're still baby bees trying to make it to the next flower, but some old-timer'll tape it, some sore dude who's been out of it for a couple of years who wants to grow. He'll smell the shit in it.

Oh
I know something about you baby
    that's sad
    don't be mad
                        baby
That you will never have children at
  rest
      at that beautiful breast
                        my love
But see
        everywhere you go, children follow you
        for more
                many more
        are the children of your life
        than the children of the married wife.

*That* one is out of the Bible, he said.

Pa, Alexandra said, don't you think a woman in this life ought to have at least one child?

No doubt about it, he said. You should have when you were married to Granofsky, the Communist. We disagreed. He had no sense of humor. He's probably boring the Cubans to death this minute. But he was an intelligent person otherwise. I would have brilliant grandchildren. They would not necessarily have the same politics.

Then he looked at her, her age and possibilities. He softened. You don't look so bad. You could still marry, dear girl. Then he softened further, thinking of hopeless statistics he had just read about the ratio of women to men. Actually! So what! It's not important, Alexandra. According to the Torah, only the man is commanded to multiply. You are not commanded. You have a child, you don't have, God doesn't care. You don't have one, you call in the maid. You say to your husband, Sweetie, get my maid with child. O.K. Well, your husband has anyway been fooling around with the maid for a couple of years, but now it's a respectable business. Good. You don't have to go through the whole thing, nine months, complications, maybe a Caesarean, no no pronto, a child for the Lord, Hosanna.

Pa, she said, several weeks later, but what if I did have a baby?

Don't be a fool, he said. Then he gave her a terrible long medical look, which included her entire body. He said, Why do you ask this question? He became red in the face, which had never happened. He took hold of his chest with his right hand, the hospital buzzer with the left. First, he said, I want the nurse! Now! Then he ordered Alexandra: marry!

Dennis said, I don't know how I got into this shit. It's not right, but because your habits and culture are different, I will compromise. What I suggest is this, Alexandra. The three children in our commune belong to us all. No one knows who the father is. It's far out. I swear—by the cock of our hard-up gods, I swear it's beautiful. One of them might be mine. But she doesn't have any distinguishing marks. Why don't you come and live with us and we'll all raise that kid up to be a decent human and humane being in this world. We need a slightly older person, we really do, with a historic sense. We lack that.

Thank you, Alexandra replied. No.

Her father said, Explain it to me, please. For what purpose did you act out this nonsense? For love? At your age. Money? Some conniver flattered you. You probably made him supper. Some starving ne'er-do-well probably wanted a few meals and said, Why not? This middle-aged fool is an easy mark. She'll give me pot roast at night, bacon and eggs in the morning.

No Pa, no, Alexandra said. Please, you'll get sicker.

John in the next bed dying with a strong heart wrote a little note to him. Doc, you're crazy. Don't leave enemies. That girl is loyal! She hasn't missed a Tues., Thurs., or Sat. Did you ever see *one* of my kids visit? Something else. I feel worse and worse. But I'm still *not ready*.

I want to tell you one more thing, her father said. You are going to embitter my last days and ruin my life.

After that, Alexandra hoped every day for her father's death, so that she could have a child without ruining his interesting life at the very end of it when ruin is absolutely retroactive.

Finally, Dennis said, Then let me at least share the pad with you. It'll be to *your* advantage.

No, Alexandra said. Please, Dennis. I've got to go to work early. I'm sleepy.

I dig. I've been a joke to you. You've used me in a bad way. That's not cool. That smells under heaven.

No, Alexandra said. Please, shut up. Anyway, how do you know you're the father?

Come on, he said, who else would be?

Alexandra smiled, bit her lip to the edge of blood to show pain politely. She was thinking about the continuity of her work, how to be proud and not lose a productive minute. She thought about the members of her case load one by one.

She said, Dennis, I know exactly what I'm going to do.

In that case, this is it, I'm splitting.

This is what Alexandra did in order to make good use of the events of her life. She invited three pregnant clients who were fifteen and sixteen years old to live with her. She visited each one and explained to them that she was pregnant too, and that her apartment was very large. Although they had disliked her because she'd always worried more about the boys, they moved out of the homes of their bad-tempered parents within a week. At the very first evening meal they began to give Alexandra good advice about men, which she did appreciate years later. She ensured their health and her own and she took notes as well. She established a precedent in social work which would not be followed or even mentioned in state journals for about five years.

Alexandra's father's life was not ruined, nor did he have to die. Shortly before the baby's birth, he fell hard on the bathroom tiles, cracked his skull, dipped the wires of his brain into his heart's blood. Short circuit! He lost twenty, thirty years in the flood, the faces of nephews, in-laws, the names of two Presidents, and a war. His eyes were rounder, he was often awestruck, but he was smart as ever, and able to begin again with fewer scruples to notice and appreciate.

The baby was born and named Dennis for his father. Of course his last name was Granofsky because of Alexandra's husband, Granofsky the Communist.

The Lepers, who had changed their name to the Edible Amanita, taped the following song in his tiny honor. It was called "Who? I."

The lyrics are simple. They are:

> Who is the father?
> Who is the father
> Who is the father
>
> I! I! I! I!
>
> I am the father
> I am the father
> I am the father.

Dennis himself sang the solo which was I! I! I! I! in a hoarse enraged prophetic voice. He had been brave to acknowledge the lyrics. After a thirty-eight-hour marathon encounter at his commune, he was asked to leave. The next afternoon he moved to a better brownstone about four blocks away where occasional fatherhood was expected.

On the baby's third birthday, Dennis and the Fair

Fields of Corn produced a folk-rock album because
that was the new sound and exciting. It was called *For
Our Son*. Tuned-in listeners could hear how taps
played by the piccolo about forty times a verse flitted
in and out of the long dark drum rolls, the ordinary
banjo chords, and the fiddle tune which was something
but not exactly like "Lullaby and Good Night."

> Will you come to see me Jack
> When I'm old and very shaky?
> Yes I will for you're my dad
> And you've lost your last old lady
> Though you traveled very far
> To the highlands and the badlands
> And ripped off the family car
> Still, old dad, I won't forsake you.

> Will you come to see me Jack?
> Though I'm really not alone.
> Still I'd like to see my boy
> For we're lonesome for our own.
> Yes I will for you're my dad
> Though you dumped me and my brothers
> And you sizzled down the road
> Loving other fellows' mothers.

> Will you come to see me Jack?
> Though I look like time boiled over.
> Growing old is not a lark.
> Yes I will for you're my dad
> Though we never saw a nickel
> As we struggled up life's ladder
> I will call you and together
> We will cuddle up and see

> What the weather's like in Key West
> On the old-age home TV.

This song was sung coast to coast and became famous from the dark Maine woods to Texas's shining gulf. It was responsible for a statistical increase in visitors to old-age homes by the apprehensive middle-aged and the astonished young.

# Politics

A group of mothers from our neighborhood went downtown to the Board of Estimate Hearing and sang a song. They had contributed the facts and the tunes, but the idea for that kind of political action came from the clever head of a media man floating on the ebbtide of our lower west side culture because of the housing shortage. He was from the far middle plains and loved our well-known tribal organization. He said it was the coming thing. Oh, how he loved our old moldy pot New York.

He was also clean-cut and attractive. For that reason the first mother stood up straight when the clerk called her name. She smiled, said excuse me, jammed past the knees of her neighbors and walked proudly down the aisle of the hearing room. Then she sang, according to some sad melody learned in her mother's kitchen, the following lament requesting better playground facilities.

oh oh oh
will someone please put a high fence
up
around the children's playground
they are playing a game and have
only

one more year of childhood. won't the city
come
or their daddies to keep the bums and
the tramps out of the yard they are too
little now to have the old men wagging their
cricked pricks at them or feeling their
knees and saying to them sweetheart
sweetheart sweetheart. can't the cardinal
keep all these creeps out . . .

She bowed her head and stepped back modestly to
allow the recitative for which all the women rose,
wherever in the hearing room they happened to be.
They said a lovely statement in chorus:

The junkies with smiles can be stopped by intelligent
reorganization of government functions.

Then she stepped forward once more, embarrassed
before the high municipal podiums and continued to
sing:

. . . please Mr. Mayor
there's a girl without any pants on    they're babies
so help me    the Commies just walk in the gate
and put shit in the sand . . .

Raising her arms toward the off-white ceiling of our
lovely City Hall, she cried out

stuff them on a freight train to Brooklyn
your honor, put up a fence
we're mothers    oh what
will become of the children . . .

No one on the Board of Estimate, including the mayor, was unimpressed. After the reiteration of the fifth singer, all the officials said so, murmuring ah and oh in a kind of startled arpeggio round lasting maybe three minutes. The comptroller, who was a famous financial nag, said, "Yes yes yes, in this case, yes, a high 16.8 fence can be put up at once, can be expedited, why not . . ." Then and there, he picked up the phone and called Parks, Traffic and Child Welfare. All were agreeable when they heard his strict voice and temperate language. By noon the next day, the fence was up.

Later that night, an hour or so past moonlight, a young Tactical Patrol Force cop snipped a good-sized hole in the fence for two reasons. The first reason was public: The Big Brothers, a baseball team of young priests who absolutely required exercise, always played at night. They needed entrance and egress. His other reason was personal: There were eleven bats locked up in the locker room. These were, to his little group, an esoteric essential. He, in fact, had already gathered them into his arms like stalks of pussywillow and loaded them into a waiting paddy wagon. He had returned for half-a-dozen catcher's mitts, when a young woman reporter from the *Lower West Side Sun* noticed him in the locker room.

She asked, because she was trained in the disciplines of curiosity followed by intelligent inquiry, what he was doing there. He replied, "A police force stripped of its power and shorn by vengeful politicians of the respect due it from the citizenry will arm itself as best it can." He had a copy of Camus's *The Rebel* in his inside pocket which he showed her for identification purposes. He had mild gray eyes, short eyelashes, a smooth and perfect countenance, white gloves of linen, barely smudged, and was able, therefore, while waiting among the basketballs for apprehension by precinct cops, to inject her with two sons, one Irish and one Italian, who sang to her in dialect all her life.

# Northeast
# Playground

the babies, though they clutched the little butterballs to their hearts or flew into the sandbox at the call of a whimper, hollering, What? What? Who? Who? Who took your shovel? Claude? Leni! Claude!

He's a real boy, said Leni.

These two didn't like to be on relief at all. They were embarrassed but not to the point of rudeness to their friends who weren't ashamed. Still, every now and then they'd make ironic remarks. They were young and very pretty, the way almost all young girls tend to be these days, and would probably never be ditched again. I tried to tell them this and they replied, Thanks! One ironic remark they'd make was, My mother says don't feel bad, Allison's a love-child. The mother was accepting and advanced, but poor.

The afternoon I visited, I asked one or two simple questions and made a statement.

I asked, Wouldn't it be better if you mixed in with the other mothers and babies who are really a friendly bunch?

They said, No.

I asked, What do you think this ghettoization will do to your children?

They smiled proudly.

Then I stated: In a way, it was like this when my children were little babies. The ladies who once wore *I Like Ike* buttons sat on the south side of the sandbox, and the rest of us who were revisionist Communist and revisionist Trotskyite and revisionist Zionist registered Democrats sat on the north side.

In response to my statement, NO kidding! most of them said.

Beat it, said Janice.

# The
# Little
# Girl

Carter stop by the café early. I just done waxing. He said, I believe I'm having company later on. Let me use your place, Charlie, hear?

I told him, Door is open, go ahead. Man coming for the meter (why I took the lock off). I told him Angie my lodger *could* be home but he strung out most the time. He don't even know when someone practicing the horn in the next room. Carter, you got hours and hours. There ain't no wine there, nothing like it. He said he had some other stuff would keep him on top. That was a joke. Thank you, brother, he said. I told him I believe I *have* tried anything, but to this day, I like whiskey. If you have whiskey, you drunk, but if you pump up with drugs, you just crazy. Yeah, hear that man, he said. Then his eyeballs start walking away.

He went right to the park. Park is full of little soft yellow-haired baby chicks. They ain't but babies. They far from home, and you better believe it, they love them big black cats walking around before lunchtime, jutting their apparatus. They think they gonna leap off that to heaven. Maybe so.

Nowadays, the spades around here got it set out for them. When I was young, *I* put that kettle to cook. *I* stirred it and stirred it. And these dudes just sucking off the gravy.

Next thing: Carter rested himself on the bench. He look this way and that. His pants is tight. His head making pictures. Along comes this child. She just straggling along. Got her big canvas pocketbook and she looking around. Carter hollers out. Hey, sit down, he says. By me, here, you pretty thing. She look sideways. Sits. On the edge.

Where you from, baby? he ask her. Hey, relax, you with friends.

Oh, thank you. Oh, the Midwest, she says. Near Chicago. She want to look good. She ain't from maybe eight hundred miles.

You left home for a visit, you little dandylion you, your boy friend let you just go?

Oh no, she says. Getting talky. I just left and for good. My mother don't let me do a thing. I got to do the breakfast dishes when I get home from school and clean and do my two brothers' room and they don't have to do nothing. And I got to be home in my room by 10 p.m. weekdays and 12 p.m. just when the fun starts Saturday and nothing is going on in that town. Nothing! It's dead, a sleeping hollow. *And the prejudice, whew!* She blushes up a little, she don't want to hurt his feelings. It's terrible and then they caught me out with a little bit of a roach I got off of some fellow from New York who was passing through and I couldn't get out at all then for a week. They was watching me and watching. They're disgusting and they're so ignorant!

My! Carter says. I don't know how you kids today stand it. The world is changing, that's a fact, and the old folks ain't heard the news. He ruffle with her hair and he lay his cheek on her hair a minute. Testing. And he puts the tip of his tongue along the tip of her ear. He's a fine-looking man, you know, a nice color, medium, not too light. Only thing wrong with him is some blood line in his eye.

I don't know when I seen a prettier chick, he says. Just what we call fattening the pussy. Which wouldn't use up no time he could see. She look at him right away, Oh Lord, I been trudging around. I am tired. Yawns.

He says, I got a nice place, you could just relax and rest and decide what to do next. Take a shower. Whatever you like. Anyways you do is O.K. My, you are sweet. You better'n Miss America. How old you say you was?

Eighteen, she jump right in.

He look at her satisfied, but that was a lie and Carter knew it, I believe. That the Number One I hold against him. Because, why her? Them little girls just flock, they do. A grown man got to use his sense.

Next thing: They set out for my apartment, which is six, seven blocks downtown. Stop for a pizza. 'Mm this is good, she says (she is so simple). She says, They don't make 'em this way back home.

They proceed. I seen Carter courting before. Canvas pocketbook across his shoulder. They holding hands maybe and hand-swinging.

Open the front door of 149, but when they through struggling up them four flights, she *got* to be disappointed, you know my place, nothing there. I got my cot. There's a table. There two chairs. Blanket on the bed. And a pillow. And a old greasy pillow slip. I'm too old now to give up my grizzily greasy head, but I sure wish I was a young buck, I would let my Afro flare *out*.

She got to be disappointed.

Wait a minute, he says, goes into the kitchen and brings back ice water, a box of pretzels. Oh, thank

you, she says. Just what I wanted. Then he says, Rest
yourself, darling and she lie down. Down, right in her
coffin.

You like to smoke? Ain't that peaceful, he says. Oh,
it is, she says. It sure is peaceful. People don't know.

Then they finish up. Just adrifting in agreement, and
he says, You like to ball? She says, Man! Do I! Then
he put up her dress and take down her panties and
tickle her here and there, nibbling away. He says, You
like that, baby? Man! I sure do, she says. A colored
boy done that to me once back home, it sure feels
good.

Right then he get off his clothes. Gonna tend to business. Now, the bad thing there is, the way Carter told
it, and I know it so, those little girls come around looking for what they used to, hot dog. And what they get
is knockwurst. You know we are like that. Matter of
fact, Carter did force her. Had to. She starting to holler, Ow, it hurts, you killing me, it hurts. But Carter
told me, it was her asked for it. Tried to get away, but
he had been stiff as stone since morning when he stop
by the store. He wasn't *about* to let her run.

Did you hit her? I said. Now Carter, I ain't gonna
tell anyone. But I got to know.

I might of hauled off and let her have it once or
twice. Stupid little cunt asked for it, didn't she? She
was so little, there wasn't enough meat on her thigh
bone to feed a sick dog. She could of wriggled by the
scoop in my armpit if I had let her. Our black women
ain't a bit like that, I told you Charlie. They cook it
up, they eat the mess they made. They proud.

I didn't let that ride too long. Carter's head moves
quick, but he don't dust me. I ask him, How come
when they passing the plate and you *is* presented with

the choice, you say like the prettiest dude, A little of that white stuff, please, man?

I don't! He hollered like I had chopped his neck. And I won't! He grab my shirt front. It was a dirty old work shirt and it tore to bits in his hand. He got solemn. Shit! You right! They are poison! They killing me! The diet gonna send me upstate for nothin but *bone* diet and I got piles as is.

Joking by the side of the grave trench. That's why I used to like him. He wasn't usual. That's why I like to pass time with Carter in the park in the early evening.

Be cool, I said.

Right on, he said.

He told me he just done shooting them little cotton-head darkies into her when Mangie Angie Emporiore lean on the doorway. Girl lying on my bloody cot pulling up a sheet, crying, bleeding out between her legs. Carter had tore her up some. You know, Charlie, he said, I ain't one of your little Jewboy buddies with half of it cut off. Angie peering and peering. Carter stood up out of his working position. He took a quick look at Angie, heisted his pants and split. He told me, Man, I couldn't stay there, that dumb cunt sniffling and that blood spreading out around her, she didn't get up to protect herself, she was disgusting, and that low white bug, your friend, crawled in from under the kitchen sink. Now on, you don't live with no white junkie, hear me Charlie, they can't use it.

Where you going now Carter? I ask him. To the pigs, he says and jabs his elbow downtown. I hear they looking for me.

That exactly what he done, and he never seen free daylight since.

Not too long that same day they came by for me. They know where I am. At the station they said, You sleep somewhere else tonight and tomorrow night. Your place padlocked. You wouldn't want to see it, Charlie. You in the clear. We know your whereabouts to the minute. Sergeant could see I didn't know nothing. Didn't want to tell me neither. I'll explain it. They had put out a warrant for Angel. Didn't want me speaking to him. Telling him anything.

Hector the beat cop over here can't keep nothing to himself. They are like that. Spanish people. Chatter chatter. What he said: You move, Charlie. You don't want to see that place again. Bed smashed in. That little girl broken up in the bottom of the airshaft on top of the garbage and busted glass. She just tossed out that toilet window wide awake alive. They know that. Death occur on ground contact.

The next day I learned worse. Hector found me outside the store. My buffer swiped. Couldn't work. He said, Every bone between her knee and her rib cage broken, splintered. She been brutally assaulted with a blunt instrument or a fist before death.

Worse than that, on her leg high up, inside, she been bitten like a animal bit her and bit her and tore her little meat she had on her. I said, All right, Hector. Shut up. Don't speak.

They put her picture in the paper every day for five days, and when her mother and daddy came on the fifth day, they said, The name of our child is Juniper. She is fourteen years old. She been a little rebellious but the kids today all like that.

Then court. I had a small job to say, Yes, it was my place. Yes, I told Carter he could use it. Yes, Angie was my roommate and sometimes he lay around there for days. He owed me two months' rent. That the reason I didn't put him out.

In court Carter said, Yes, I did force her, but he said he didn't do nothing else.

Angie said, I did smack her when I seen what she done, but I never bit her, your honor, I ain't no animal, that black hippie must of.

Nobody said—they couldn't drag out of anyone—they lacking the evidence who it was picked her up like she was nothing, a bag of busted bones, and dumped her out the fifth-floor window.

But wasn't it a shame, them two studs. Why they take it out on her? After so many fluffy little chicks. They could of played her easy. Why Carter seen it many times hisself. She could of stayed the summer. We just like the UN. Every state in the union stop by. She would of got her higher education right on the fifth-floor front. September, her mama and daddy would come for her and they whip her bottom, we know that. We been in the world long enough. We seen lots of the little girls. They go home, then after a while they get to be grown womens, they integrating the swimming pool and picketing the supermarket, they blink their eyes and shut their mouth and grin.

But that was my room and my bed, so I don't forget it. I don't stop thinking, That child . . . That child . . . And it come to me yesterday, I lay down after work: Maybe it wasn't no one. Maybe she pull herself the way she was, crumpled, to that open window. She was tore up, she must of thought she was gutted inside her skin. She must of been in a horror what she got to remember—what her folks would see. Her life look to be disgusting like a squashed fish, so what she did: she made up some power somehow and raise herself up that windowsill and hook herself onto it and then what I see, she just topple herself out. That what I think right now.

That is what happened.

# A
Conversation
with My
Father

My father is eighty-six years old and in bed. His heart, that bloody motor, is equally old and will not do certain jobs any more. It still floods his head with brainy light. But it won't let his legs carry the weight of his body around the house. Despite my metaphors, this muscle failure is not due to his old heart, he says, but to a potassium shortage. Sitting on one pillow, leaning on three, he offers last-minute advice and makes a request.

"I would like you to write a simple story just once more," he says, "the kind de Maupassant wrote, or Chekhov, the kind you used to write. Just recognizable people and then write down what happened to them next."

I say, "Yes, why not? That's possible." I want to please him, though I don't remember writing that way. I *would* like to try to tell such a story, if he means the kind that begins: "There was a woman . . ." followed by plot, the absolute line between two points which I've always despised. Not for literary reasons, but because it takes all hope away. Everyone, real or invented, deserves the open destiny of life.

Finally I thought of a story that had been happening for a couple of years right across the street. I wrote it down, then read it aloud. "Pa," I said, "how about this? Do you mean something like this?"

Once in my time there was a woman and she had a son. They lived nicely, in a small apartment in Manhattan. This boy at about fifteen became a junkie, which is not unusual in our neighborhood. In order to maintain her close friendship with him, she became a junkie too. She said it was part of the youth culture, with which she felt very much at home. After a while, for a number of reasons, the boy gave it all up and left the city and his mother in disgust. Hopeless and alone, she grieved. We all visit her.

"O.K., Pa, that's it," I said, "an unadorned and miserable tale."

"But that's not what I mean," my father said. "You misunderstood me on purpose. You know there's a lot more to it. You know that. You left everything out. Turgenev wouldn't do that. Chekhov wouldn't do that. There are in fact Russian writers you never heard of, you don't have an inkling of, as good as anyone, who can write a plain ordinary story, who would not leave out what you have left out. I object not to facts but to people sitting in trees talking senselessly, voices from who knows where . . ."

"Forget that one, Pa, what have I left out now? In this one?"

"Her looks, for instance."

"Oh. Quite handsome, I think. Yes."

"Her hair?"

"Dark, with heavy braids, as though she were a girl or a foreigner."

"What were her parents like, her stock? That she became such a person. It's interesting, you know."

"From out of town. Professional people. The first to be divorced in their county. How's that? Enough?" I asked.

"With you, it's all a joke," he said. "What about the boy's father? Why didn't you mention him? Who was he? Or was the boy born out of wedlock?"

"Yes," I said. "He was born out of wedlock."

"For Godsakes, doesn't anyone in your stories get married? Doesn't anyone have the time to run down to City Hall before they jump into bed?"

"No," I said. "In real life, yes. But in my stories, no."

"Why do you answer me like that?"

"Oh, Pa, this is a simple story about a smart woman who came to N.Y.C. full of interest love trust excitement very up to date, and about her son, what a hard time she had in this world. Married or not, it's of small consequence."

"It is of great consequence," he said.

"O.K.," I said.

"O.K. O.K. yourself," he said, "but listen. I believe you that she's good-looking, but I don't think she was so smart."

"That's true," I said. "Actually that's the trouble with stories. People start out fantastic. You think they're extraordinary, but it turns out as the work goes along, they're just average with a good education. Sometimes the other way around, the person's a kind of dumb innocent, but he outwits you and you can't even think of an ending good enough."

"What do you do then?" he asked. He had been a doctor for a couple of decades and then an artist for a couple of decades and he's still interested in details, craft, technique.

"Well, you just have to let the story lie around till

some agreement can be reached between you and the stubborn hero."

"Aren't you talking silly, now?" he asked. "Start again," he said. "It so happens I'm not going out this evening. Tell the story again. See what you can do this time."

"O.K.," I said. "But it's not a five-minute job." Second attempt:

> Once, across the street from us, there was a fine handsome woman, our neighbor. She had a son whom she loved because she'd known him since birth (in helpless chubby infancy, and in the wrestling, hugging ages, seven to ten, as well as earlier and later). This boy, when he fell into the fist of adolescence, became a junkie. He was not a hopeless one. He was in fact hopeful, an ideologue and successful converter. With his busy brilliance, he wrote persuasive articles for his high-school newspaper. Seeking a wider audience, using important connections, he drummed into Lower Manhattan newsstand distribution a periodical called *Oh! Golden Horse!*
>
> In order to keep him from feeling guilty (because guilt is the stony heart of nine tenths of all clinically diagnosed cancers in America today, she said), and because she had always believed in giving bad habits room at home where one could keep an eye on them, she too became a junkie. Her kitchen was famous for a while—a center for intellectual addicts who knew what they were doing. A few felt artistic like Coleridge and others were scientific and revolutionary like Leary. Although she was often high herself, certain good mothering reflexes remained, and she saw to it

that there was lots of orange juice around and honey and milk and vitamin pills. However, she never cooked anything but chili, and that no more than once a week. She explained, when we talked to her, seriously, with neighborly concern, that it was her part in the youth culture and she would rather be with the young, it was an honor, than with her own generation.

One week, while nodding through an Antonioni film, this boy was severely jabbed by the elbow of a stern and proselytizing girl, sitting beside him. She offered immediate apricots and nuts for his sugar level, spoke to him sharply, and took him home.

She had heard of him and his work and she herself published, edited, and wrote a competitive journal called *Man Does Live By Bread Alone*. In the organic heat of her continuous presence he could not help but become interested once more in his muscles, his arteries, and nerve connections. In fact he began to love them, treasure them, praise them with funny little songs in *Man Does Live* . . .

> the fingers of my flesh transcend
> my transcendental soul
> the tightness in my shoulders end
> my teeth have made me whole

To the mouth of his head (that glory of will and determination) he brought hard apples, nuts, wheat germ, and soybean oil. He said to his old friends, From now on, I guess I'll keep my wits about me. I'm going on the natch. He said he was about to begin a spiritual deep-breathing journey.

How about you too, Mom? he asked kindly.

His conversion was so radiant, splendid, that
neighborhood kids his age began to say that he had
never been a real addict at all, only a journalist
along for the smell of the story. The mother tried
several times to give up what had become without her son and his friends a lonely habit. This effort only brought it to supportable levels. The boy
and his girl took their electronic mimeograph and
moved to the bushy edge of another borough. They
were very strict. They said they would not see her
again until she had been off drugs for sixty days.

At home alone in the evening, weeping, the
mother read and reread the seven issues of *Oh!
Golden Horse!* They seemed to her as truthful as
ever. We often crossed the street to visit and con-
sole. But if we mentioned any of our children who
were at college or in the hospital or dropouts at
home, she would cry out, My baby! My baby! and
burst into terrible, face-scarring, time-consuming
tears. The End.

First my father was silent, then he said, "Number
One: You have a nice sense of humor. Number Two:
I see you can't tell a plain story. So don't waste time."
Then he said sadly, "Number Three: I suppose that
means she was alone, she was left like that, his mother.
Alone. Probably sick?"

I said, "Yes."

"Poor woman. Poor girl, to be born in a time of
fools, to live among fools. The end. The end. You were
right to put that down. The end."

I didn't want to argue, but I had to say, "Well, it is
not necessarily the end, Pa."

"Yes," he said, "what a tragedy. The end of a person."

"No, Pa," I begged him. "It doesn't have to be. She's only about forty. She could be a hundred different things in this world as time goes on. A teacher or a social worker. An ex-junkie! Sometimes it's better than having a master's in education."

"Jokes," he said. "As a writer that's your main trouble. You don't want to recognize it. Tragedy! Plain tragedy! Historical tragedy! No hope. The end."

"Oh, Pa," I said. "She could change."

"In your own life, too, you have to look it in the face." He took a couple of nitroglycerin. "Turn to five," he said, pointing to the dial on the oxygen tank. He inserted the tubes into his nostrils and breathed deep. He closed his eyes and said, "No."

I had promised the family to always let him have the last word when arguing, but in this case I had a different responsibility. That woman lives across the street. She's my knowledge and my invention. I'm sorry for her. I'm not going to leave her there in that house crying. (Actually neither would Life, which unlike me has no pity.)

Therefore: She did change. Of course her son never came home again. But right now, she's the receptionist in a storefront community clinic in the East Village. Most of the customers are young people, some old friends. The head doctor has said to her, "If we only had three people in this clinic with your experiences . . ."

"The doctor said that?" My father took the oxygen tubes out of his nostrils and said, "Jokes. Jokes again."

"No, Pa, it could really happen that way, it's a funny world nowadays."

"No," he said. "Truth first. She will slide back. A person must have character. She does not."

"No, Pa," I said. "That's it. She's got a job. Forget it. She's in that storefront working."

"How long will it be?" he asked. "Tragedy! You too. When will you look it in the face?"

# The
# Immigrant
# Story

Jack asked me, Isn't it a terrible thing to grow up in the shadow of another person's sorrow?

I suppose so, I answered. As you know, I grew up in the summer sunlight of upward mobility. This leached out a lot of that dark ancestral grief.

He went on with *his* life. It's not your fault if that's the case. Your bad disposition is not your fault. Yet you're always angry. No way out but continuous rage or the nuthouse.

What if this sorrow is all due to history? I asked.

The cruel history of Europe, he said. In this way he showed ironic respect to one of my known themes.

The whole world ought to be opposed to Europe for its cruel history, Jack, and yet in favor of it because after about a thousand years it may have learned some sense.

Nonsense, he said objectively, a thousand years of outgoing persistent imperial cruelty tends to make enemies and if all you have to deal with these enemies is good sense, what then?

My dear, no one knows the power of good sense. It hasn't been built up or experimented with sufficiently.

I'm trying to tell you something, he said. Listen. One day I woke up and my father was asleep in the crib.

I wonder why, I said.

My mother made him sleep in the crib.

All the time?

That time anyway. That time I saw him.

I wonder why, I said.

Because she didn't want him to fuck her, he said.

No, I don't believe that. Who told you that?

I know it! He pointed his finger at me.

I don't believe it, I said. Unless she's had five babies all in a row or they have to get up at 6 a.m. or they both hate each other, most people like their husbands to do that.

Bullshit! She was trying to make him feel guilty. Where were his balls?

I will never respond to that question. Asked in a worried way again and again, it may become responsible for the destruction of the entire world. I gave it two minutes of silence.

He said, Misery misery misery. Grayness. I see it all very very gray. My mother approaches the crib. Shmul, she says, get up. Run down to the corner and get me half a pound of pot cheese. Then run over the drugstore and get a few ounces cod-liver oil. My father, scrunched like an old gray fetus, looks up and smiles smiles smiles at the bitch.

How do *you* know what was going on? I asked. You were five years old.

What do you think was going on?

I'll tell you. It's not so hard. Any dope who's had a normal life could tell you. Anyone whose head hasn't been fermenting with the compost of ten years of gluttonous analysis. Anyone could tell you.

Tell me what? he screamed.

The reason your father was sleeping in the crib was that you and your sister who usually slept in the crib had scarlet fever and needed the decent beds and more room to sweat, come to a fever crisis, and either get well or die.

Who told you that? He lunged at me as though I was an enemy.

You fucking enemy, he said. You always see things in a rosy light. You have a rotten rosy temperament. You were like that in sixth grade. One day you brought three American flags to school.

That was true. I made an announcement to the sixth-grade assembly thirty years ago. I said: I thank God every day that I'm not in Europe. I thank God I'm American-born and live on East 172nd Street where there is a grocery store, a candy store, and a drugstore on one corner and on the same block a shul and two doctors' offices.

One Hundred and Seventy-second Street was a pile of shit, he said. Everyone was on relief except you. Thirty people had t.b. Citizens and noncitizens alike starving until the war. Thank God capitalism has a war it can pull out of the old feed bag every now and then or we'd all be dead. Ha ha.

I'm glad that you're not totally brainwashed by stocks, bonds, and cash. I'm glad to hear you still mention capitalism from time to time.

Because of poverty, brilliance, and the early appearance of lots of soft hair on face and crotch, my friend Jack was a noticeable Marxist and Freudian by the morning of his twelfth birthday.

In fact, his mind thickened with ideas. I continued to put out more flags. There were twenty-eight flags aflutter in different rooms and windows. I had one tattooed onto my arm. It has gotten dimmer but a lot wider because of middle age.

I am probably more radical than you are nowadays,

I said. Since I was not wiped out of my profession during the McCarthy inquisitions, I therefore did not have to go into business for myself and make a fortune. (Naturally many have remained wiped out to this day, gifted engineers and affectionate teachers . . . This makes me think often of courage and loyalty.)

I believe I see the world as clearly as you do, I said. Rosiness is not a worse windowpane than gloomy gray when viewing the world.

Yes yes yes yes yes yes yes, he said. Do you mind? Just listen:

My mother and father came from a small town in Poland. They had three sons. My father decided to go to America, to 1. stay out of the army, 2. stay out of jail, 3. save his children from everyday wars and ordinary pogroms. He was helped by the savings of parents, uncles, grandmothers and set off like hundreds of thousands of others in that year. In America, New York City, he lived a hard but hopeful life. Sometimes he walked on Delancey Street. Sometimes like a bachelor he went to the theater on Second Avenue. Mostly he put his money away for the day he could bring his wife and sons to this place. Meanwhile, in Poland famine struck. Not hunger which all Americans suffer six, seven times a day but Famine, which tells the body to consume itself. First the fat, then the meat, the muscle, then the blood. Famine ate up the bodies of the little boys pretty quickly. My father met my mother at the boat. He looked at her face, her hands. There was no baby in her arms, no children dragging at her skirt. She was not wearing her hair in two long black braids. There was a kerchief over a dark wiry wig. She had shaved her head, like a backward Orthodox bride, though they had been serious advanced socialists like most of the youth of their town. He took her by the hand and brought her home. They never went anywhere alone, except to work or the grocer's. They held each other's hand when they sat down at the table, even at breakfast. Sometimes he patted her hand, sometimes she patted his. He read the paper to her every night.

They are sitting at the edge of their chairs. He's leaning forward reading to her in that old bulb light. Sometimes she smiles just a little. Then he puts the paper down and takes both her hands in his as though they needed warmth. He continues to read. Just beyond the table and their heads, there is the darkness of the kitchen, the bedroom, the dining room, the shadowy darkness where as a child I ate my supper, did my homework and went to bed.

# The Long-Distance Runner

One day, before or after forty-two, I became a long-distance runner. Though I was stout and in many ways inadequate to this desire, I wanted to go far and fast, not as fast as bicycles and trains, not as far as Taipei, Hingwen, places like that, islands of the slant-eyed cunt, as sailors in bus stations say when speaking of travel, but round and round the county from the sea side to the bridges, along the old neighborhood streets a couple of times, before old age and urban renewal ended them and me.

I tried the country first, Connecticut, which being wooded is always full of buds in spring. All creation is secret, isn't that true? So I trained in the wide-zoned suburban hills where I wasn't known. I ran all spring in and out of dogwood bloom, then laurel.

People sometimes stopped and asked me why I ran, a lady in silk shorts halfway down over her fat thighs. In training, I replied and rested only to answer if closely questioned. I wore a white sleeveless undershirt as well, with excellent support, not to attract the attention of old men and prudish children.

Then summer came, my legs seemed strong. I kissed the kids goodbye. They were quite old by then. It was near the time for parting anyway. I told Mrs. Raftery to look in now and then and give them some of that rotten Celtic supper she makes.

I told them they could take off any time they wanted to. Go lead your private life, I said. Only leave me out of it.

A word to the wise . . . said Richard.

You're depressed Faith, Mrs. Raftery said. Your boy friend Jack, the one you think's so hotsy-totsy, hasn't called and you're as gloomy as a tick on Sunday.

Cut the folkshit with me, Raftery, I muttered. Her eyes filled with tears because that's who she is: folk-shit from bunion to topknot. That's how she got liked by me, loved, invented and endured.

When I walked out the door they were all reclining before the television set, Richard, Tonto and Mrs. Raftery, gazing at the news. Which proved with moving pictures that there *had* been a voyage to the moon and Africa and South America hid in a furious whorl of clouds.

I said, Goodbye. They said, Yeah, O.K., sure.

If that's how it is, forget it, I hollered and took the Independent subway to Brighton Beach.

At Brighton Beach I stopped at the Salty Breezes Locker Room to change my clothes. Twenty-five years ago my father invested $500 in its future. In fact he still clears about $3.50 a year, which goes directly (by law) to the Children of Judea to cover their deficit.

No one paid too much attention when I started to run, easy and light on my feet. I ran on the boardwalk first, past my mother's leafleting station—between a soft-ice-cream stand and a degenerated dune. There she had been assigned by her comrades to halt the tides of cruel American enterprise with simple socialist sense.

I wanted to stop and admire the long beach. I wanted to stop in order to think admiringly about New York.

There aren't many rotting cities so tan and sandy and speckled with citizens at their salty edges. But I had already spent a lot of life lying down or standing and staring. I had decided to run.

After about a mile and a half I left the boardwalk and began to trot into the old neighborhood. I was running well. My breath was long and deep. I was thinking pridefully about my form.

Suddenly I was surrounded by about three hundred blacks.

Who you?

Who that?

Look at her! Just look! When you seen a fatter ass?

Poor thing. She ain't right. Leave her, you boys, you bad boys.

I used to live here, I said.

Oh yes, they said, in the white old days. That time too bad to last.

But we loved it here. We never went to Flatbush Avenue or Times Square. We loved our block.

Tough black titty.

I like your speech, I said. Metaphor and all.

Right on. We get that from talking.

Yes my people also had a way of speech. And don't forget the Irish. The gift of gab.

Who they? said a small boy.

Cops.

Nowadays, I suggested, there's more than Irish on the police force.

You right, said two ladies. More, more, much much more. They's French Chinamen Russkies Congoleans. Oh missee, you too right.

I lived in that house, I said. That apartment house. All my life. Till I got married.

Now that *is* nice. Live in one place. My mother live
that way in South Carolina. One place. Her daddy
farmed. She said. They ate. No matter winter war bad
times. Roosevelt. Something! Ain't that wonderful! And
it weren't cold! Big trees!

*That* apartment. I looked up and pointed. There.
The third floor.

They all looked up. So what! You blubrous devil!
said a dark young man. He wore horn-rimmed glasses
and had that intelligent look that City College boys
used to have when I was eighteen and first looked at
them.

He seemed to lead them in contempt and anger,
even the littlest ones who moved toward me with dra-
matic stealth singing, Devil, Oh Devil. I don't think the
little kids had bad feeling because they poked a finger
into me, then laughed.

Still I thought it might be wise to keep my head. So I
jumped right in with some facts. I said, How many
flowers' names do you know? Wild flowers, I mean. My
people only knew two. That's what they say now anyway. Rich or poor, they only had two flowers' names.
Rose and violet.

Daisy, said one boy immediately.

Weed, said another. That *is* a flower, I thought. But
everyone else got the joke.

Saxifrage, lupine, said a lady. Viper's bugloss, said
a small Girl Scout in medium green with a dark green
sash. She held up a *Handbook of Wild Flowers*.

How many you know, fat mama? a boy asked warm-
ly. He wasn't against my being a mother or fat. I
turned all my attention to him.

Oh sonny, I said, I'm way ahead of my people. I
know in yellows alone: common cinquefoil, trout lily,

yellow adder's-tongue, swamp buttercup and common buttercup, golden sorrel, yellow or hop clover, devil's-paintbrush, evening primrose, black-eyed Susan, golden aster, also the yellow pickerelweed growing down by the water if not in the water, and dandelions of course. I've seen all these myself. Seen them.

You could see China from the boardwalk, a boy said. When it's nice.

I know more flowers than countries. Mostly young people these days have traveled in many countries.

Not me. I ain't been nowhere.

Not me either, said about seventeen boys.

*I'm* not allowed, said a little girl. There's drunken junkies.

But *I! I!* cried out a tall black youth, very handsome and well dressed. I am an African. My father came from the high stolen plains. *I* have been everywhere. I was in Moscow six months, learning machinery. I was in France, learning French. I was in Italy, observing the peculiar Renaissance and the people's sweetness. I was in England, where I studied the common law and the urban blight. I was at the Conference of Dark Youth in Cuba to understand our passion. I am now here. Here am I to become an engineer and return to my people, around the Cape of Good Hope in a Norwegian sailing vessel. In this way I will learn the fine old art of sailing in case the engines of the new society of my old inland country should fail.

We had an extraordinary amount of silence after that. Then one old lady in a black dress and high white lace collar said to another old lady dressed exactly the same way, Glad tidings when someone got brains in the head not fish juice. Amen, said a few.

Whyn't you go up to Mrs. Luddy living in your

house, you lady, huh? The Girl Scout asked this.

Why she just groove to see you, said some sarcastic snickerer.

She got palpitations. Her man, he give it to her.

That ain't all, he a natural gift-giver.

I'll take you, said the Girl Scout. My name is Cynthia. I'm in Troop 355, Brooklyn.

I'm not dressed, I said, looking at my lumpy knees.

You shouldn't wear no undershirt like that without no runnin number or no team writ on it. It look like a undershirt.

Cynthia! Don't take her up there, said an important boy. Her head strange. Don't you take her. Hear?

Lawrence, she said softly, you tell me once more what to do I'll wrap you round that lamppost.

Git! she said, powerfully addressing *me*.

In this way I was led into the hallway of the whole house of my childhood.


The first door I saw was still marked in flaky gold, 1A. That's where the janitor lived, I said. He was a Negro.

How come like that? Cynthia made an astonished face. How come the janitor was a black man?

Oh Cynthia, I said. Then I turned to the opposite door, first floor front, 1B. I remembered. Now, here, this was Mrs. Goreditsky, very very fat lady. All her children died at birth. Born, then one, two, three. Dead. Five children, then Mr. Goreditsky said, I'm bad luck on you Tessie and he went away. He sent $15 a week for seven years. Then no one heard.

I know her, poor thing, said Cynthia. The city come for her summer before last. The way they knew, it smelled. They wropped her up in a canvas. They couldn't get through the front door. It scraped off a piece of her. My uncle Ronald had to help them, but he got disgusted.

Only two years ago. She was still here! Wasn't she scared?

So we all, said Cynthia. White ain't everything.

Who lived up here, she asked, 2B? Right now, my best friend Nancy Rosalind lives here. She got two brothers, and her sister married and got a baby. She very light-skinned. Not her mother. We got all colors amongst us.

Your best friend? That's funny. Because it was *my* best friend. Right in that apartment. Joanna Rosen.

What become of her? Cynthia asked. She got a running shirt too?

Come on Cynthia, if you really want to know, I'll tell you. She married this man, Marvin Steirs.

Who's he?

I recollected his achievements. Well, he's the president of a big corporation, JoMar Plastics. This corporation owns a steel company, a radio station, a new Xerox-type machine that lets you do twenty-five different pages at once. This corporation has a foundation, The JoMar Fund for Research in Conservation. Capitalism is like that, I added, in order to be politically useful.

How come you know? You go over their house a lot?

No. I happened to read all about them on the financial page, just last week. It made me think: a different life. That's all.

Different spokes for different folks, said Cynthia.

I sat down on the cool marble steps and remembered Joanna's cousin Ziggie. He was older than we were. He wrote a poem which told us we were lovely flowers

and our legs were petals, which nature would force open
no matter how many times we said no.

Then I had several other interior thoughts that I
couldn't share with a child, the kind that give your face
a blank or melancholy look.

Now you're not interested, said Cynthia. Now you're
not gonna say a thing. Who lived here, 2A? Who? Two
men lives here now. Women coming and women going.
My mother says, Danger sign: Stay away, my darling,
stay away.

I don't remember, Cynthia. I really don't.

You got to. What'd you come for, anyways?

Then I tried. 2A. 2A. Was it the twins? I felt a
strong obligation as though remembering was in charge
of the *existence* of the past. This is not so.

Cynthia, I said, I don't want to go any further. I
don't even want to remember.

Come on, she said, tugging at my shorts, don't you
want to see Mrs. Luddy, the one lives in your old
house? That be fun, no?

No. No, I don't want to see Mrs. Luddy.

Now you shouldn't pay no attention to those boys
downstairs. She will like you. I mean, she is kind. She
don't like most white people, but she might like you.

No Cynthia, it's not that, but I don't want to see
my father and mother's house now.

I didn't know what to say. I said, Because my
mother's dead. This was a lie, because my mother lives
in her own room with my father in the Children of
Judea. With her hand over her socialist heart, she reads
the paper every morning after breakfast. Then she
says sadly to my father, Every day the same. Dying . . .
dying, dying from killing.

My mother's dead Cynthia. I can't go in there.

Oh . . . oh, the poor thing, she said, looking into my

eyes. Oh, if my mother died, I don't know what I'd do. Even if I was old as you. I could kill myself. Tears filled her eyes and started down her cheeks. If my mother died, what would I do? She is my protector, she won't let the pushers get me. She hold me tight. She gonna hide me in the cedar box if my Uncle Rudford comes try to get me back. She *can't* die, my mother.

Cynthia—honey—she won't die. She's young. I put my arm out to comfort her. You could come live with me, I said. I got two boys, they're nearly grown up. I missed it, not having a girl.

What? What you mean now, live with you and boys. She pulled away and ran for the stairs. Stay way from me, honky lady. I know them white boys. They just gonna try and jostle my black womanhood. My mother told me about that, keep you white honky devil boys to your devil self, you just leave me be you old bitch you. Somebody help me, she started to scream, you hear. Somebody help. She gonna take me away.

She flattened herself to the wall, trembling. I was too frightened by her fear of me to say, honey, I wouldn't hurt you, it's me. I heard her helpers, the voices of large boys crying. We coming, we coming, hold your head up, we coming. I ran past her fear to the stairs and up them two at a time. I came to my old own door. I knocked like the landlord, loud and terrible.

Mama not home, a child's voice said. No, no, I said. It's me! a lady! Someone's chasing me, let me in. Mama not home, I ain't allowed to open up for nobody.

It's me! I cried out in terror. Mama! Mama! let me in!

The door opened. A slim woman whose age I couldn't invent looked at me. She said, Get in and shut that door tight. She took a hard pinching hold on my

upper arm. Then she bolted the door herself. Them
hustlers after you. They make me pink. Hide this
white lady now, Donald. Stick her under your bed,
you got a high bed.

Oh that's O.K. I'm fine now, I said. I felt safe and
at home.

You in my house, she said. You do as I say. For two
cents, I throw you out.

I squatted under a small kid's pissy mattress. Then I
heard the knock. It was tentative and respectful. My
mama don't allow me to open. Donald! someone called.
Donald!

Oh no, he said. Can't do it. She gonna wear me
out. You know her. She already tore up my ass this
morning once. Ain't *gonna* open up.

I lived there for about three weeks with Mrs. Luddy
and Donald and three little baby girls nearly the same
age. I told her a joke about Irish twins. Ain't Irish, she
said.

Nearly every morning the babies woke us at about
6:45. We gave them all a bottle and went back to sleep
till 8:00. I made coffee and she changed diapers. Then
it really stank for a while. At this time I usually said,
Well listen, thanks really, but I've got to go I guess. I
guess I'm going. She'd usually say, Well, guess again.
*I* guess you ain't. Or if she was feeling disgusted she'd
say, Go on now! Get! You wanna go, I guess by now
I have snorted enough white lady stink to choke a
horse. Go on!

I'd get to the door and then I'd hear voices. I'm
ashamed to say I'd become fearful. Despite my wide
geographical love of mankind, I would be attacked by
local fears.

There was a sentimental truth that lay beside all that going and not going. It *was* my house where I'd lived long ago my family life. There was a tile on the bathroom floor that I myself had broken, dropping a hammer on the toe of my brother Charles as he stood dreamily shaving, his prick halfway up his undershorts. Astonishment and knowledge first seized me right there. The kitchen was the same. The table was the enameled table common to our class, easy to clean, with wooden undercorners for indigent and old cockroaches that couldn't make it to the kitchen sink. (However, it was not the same table, because I have inherited that one, chips and all.)

The living room was something like ours, only we had less plastic. There may have been less plastic in the world at that time. Also, my mother had set beautiful cushions everywhere, on beds and chairs. It was the way she expressed herself, artistically, to embroider at night or take strips of flowered cotton and sew them across ordinary white or blue muslin in the most delicate designs, the way women have always used materials that live and die in hunks and tatters to say: This is my place.

Mrs. Luddy said, Uh huh!

Of course, I said, men don't have that outlet. That's how come they run around so much.

Till they drunk enough to lay down, she said.

Yes, I said, on a large scale you can see it in the world. First they make something, then they murder it. Then they write a book about how interesting it is.

You got something there, she said. Sometimes she said, Girl, you don't know *nothing*.

We often sat at the window looking out and down. Little tufts of breeze grew on that windowsill. The blazing afternoon was around the corner and up the block.

You say men, she said. Is that men? she asked.
What you call—a Man?

Four flights below us, leaning on the stoop, were
about a dozen people and around them devastation.
Just a minute, I said. I had seen devastation on my
way, running, gotten some of the pebbles of it in my
running shoe and the dust of it in my eyes. I had
thought with the indignant courtesy of a citizen, This
is a disgrace to the City of New York which I love and
am running through.

But now, from the commanding heights of home, I
saw it clearly. The tenement in which Jack my old and
present friend had come to gloomy manhood had been
destroyed, first by fire, then by demolition (which is a
swinging ball of steel that cracks bedrooms and kitch-
ens). Because of this work, we could see several blocks
wide and a block and a half long. Crazy Eddy's house
still stood, famous 1510 gutted, with black window
frames, no glass, open laths. The stubbornness of the
supporting beams! Some persons or families still lived
on the lowest floors. In the lots between, a couple of
old sofas lay on their fat faces, their springs sticking
up into the air. Just as in wartime a half-dozen ailanthus
trees had already found their first quarter inch of
earth and begun a living attack on the dead yards. At
night, I knew animals roamed the place, squalling and
howling, furious New York dogs and street cats and
mighty rats. You would think you were in Bear Mountain Park, the terror of venturing forth.

Someone ought to clean that up, I said.

Mrs. Luddy said, Who you got in mind? Mrs.
Kennedy?—

Donald made a stern face. He said, That just what I
gonna do when I get big. Gonna get the Sanitary Man

in and show it to him. You see that, you big guinea you, you clean it up right now! Then he stamped his feet and fierced his eyes.

Mrs. Luddy said, Come here, you little nigger. She kissed the top of his head and gave him a whack on the backside all at one time.

Well, said Donald, encouraged, look out there now you all! Go on I say, look! Though we had already seen, to please him we looked. So the stoop men and boys lounged, leaned, hopped about, stood on one leg, then another, took their socks off, and scratched their toes, talked, sat on their haunches, heads down, dozing.

Donald said, Look at them. They ain't got self-respect. They got Afros *on* their heads, but they don't know they black *in* their heads.

I thought he ought to learn to be more sympathetic. I said, There are reasons that people are that way.

Yes, ma'am, said Donald.

Anyway, how come you never go down and play with the other kids, how come you're up here so much?

My mama don't like me do that. Some of them is bad. Bad. I might become a dope addict. I got to stay clear.

You just a dope, that's a fact, said Mrs. Luddy.

He ought to be with kids his age more, I think.

He see them in school, miss. Don't trouble your head about it if you don't mind.

Actually, Mrs. Luddy didn't go down into the street either. Donald did all the shopping. She let the welfare investigator in, the meterman came into the kitchen to read the meter. I saw him from the back room, where I hid. She did pick up her check. She cashed it. She returned to wash the babies, change their diapers, wash clothes, iron, feed people, and then in free half hours she sat by that window. She was waiting.

I believed she was watching and waiting for a particular man. I wanted to discuss this with her, talk lovingly like sisters. But before I could freely say, Forget about that son of a bitch, he's a pig, I did have to offer a few solid facts about myself, my kids, about fathers, husbands, passers-by, evening companions, and the life of my father and mother in this room by this exact afternoon window.

I told her for instance, that in my worst times I had given myself one extremely simple physical pleasure. This was cream cheese for breakfast. In fact, I insisted on it, sometimes depriving the children of very important articles and foods.

Girl, you don't know nothing, she said.

Then for a little while she talked gently as one does to a person who is innocent and insane and incorruptible because of stupidity. She had had two such special pleasures for hard times she said. The first, men, but they turned rotten, white women had ruined the best, give them the idea their dicks made of solid gold. The second pleasure she had tried was wine. She said, I do like wine. You *has* to have something just for yourself by yourself. Then she said, But you can't raise a decent boy when you liquor-dazed every night.

White or black, I said, returning to men, they did think they were bringing a rare gift, whereas it was just sex, which is common like bread, though essential.

Oh, you can do without, she said. There's folks does without.

I told her Donald deserved the best. I loved him. If he had flaws, I hardly noticed them. It's one of my beliefs that children do not have flaws, even the worst do not.

Donald was brilliant—like my boys except that he had an easier disposition. For this reason I decided, almost the second moment of my residence in that household, to bring him up to reading level at once. I told him we would work with books and newspapers. He went immediately to his neighborhood library and brought some hard books to amuse me. *Black Folktales* by Julius Lester and *The Pushcart War,* which is about another neighborhood but relevant.

Donald always agreed with me when we talked about reading and writing. In fact, when I mentioned poetry, he told me he knew all about it, that David Henderson, a known black poet, had visited his second-grade class. So Donald was, as it turned out, well ahead of my nosy tongue. He was usually very busy shopping. He also had to spend a lot of time making faces to force the little serious baby girls into laughter. But if the subject came up, he could take *the* poem right out of the air into which language and event had just gone.

An example: That morning, his mother had said, Whew, I just got too much piss and diapers and wash. I wanna just sit down by that window and rest myself. He wrote a poem:

> Just got too much pissy diapers
> and wash and wash
> just wanna sit down by that window
> and look out
>        ain't nothing there.

Donald, I said, you are plain brilliant. I'm never going to forget you. For God's sakes don't you forget me.

You fool with him too much, said Mrs. Luddy. He already don't even remember his grandma, you never

gonna meet someone like her, a curse never come past
her lips.

I do remember, Mama, I remember. She lying in
bed, right there. A man standing in the door. She say,
Esdras, I put a curse on you head. You worsen tomorrow. How come she said like that?

Gomorrah, I believe Gomorrah, she said. She know
the Bible inside out.

Did she live with you?

No. No, she visiting. She come up to see us all, her
children, how we doing. She come up to see sights.
Then she lay down and died. She was old.

I remained quiet because of the death of mothers.
Mrs. Luddy looked at me thoughtfully, then she said:

My mama had stories to tell, she raised me on. *Her*
mama was a little thing, no sense. Stand in the door of
the cabin all day, sucking her thumb. It was slave
times. One day a young field boy come storming along.
He knock on the door of the first cabin hollering, Sister, come out, it's freedom. She come out. She say,
Yeah? When? He say, Now! It's freedom now! Then
he knock at the next door and say, Sister! It's freedom!
Now! From one cabin he run to the next cabin, crying out, Sister, it's freedom now!

Oh I remember that story, said Donald. Freedom
now! Freedom now! He jumped up and down.

You don't remember nothing boy. Go on, get Eloise,
she want to get into the good times.

Eloise was two but undersized. We got her like that,
said Donald. Mrs. Luddy let me buy her ice cream
and green vegetables. She was waiting for kale and
chard, but it was too early. The kale liked cold. You
not about to be here November, she said. No, no. I
turned away, lonesomeness touching me and sang our
Eloise song:

> Eloise loves the bees
> the bees they buzz
> like Eloise does.

Then Eloise crawled all over the splintery floor, buzzing wildly.

Oh you crazy baby, said Donald, buzz buzz buzz.

Mrs. Luddy sat down by the window.

You all make a lot of noise, she said sadly. You just right on noisy.

The next morning Mrs. Luddy woke me up.

Time to go, she said.

What?

Home.

What? I said.

Well, don't you think your little spoiled boys crying for you? Where's Mama? They standing in the window. Time to go lady. This ain't Free Vacation Farm. Time we was by ourself a little.

Oh Ma, said Donald, she ain't a lot of trouble. Go on, get Eloise, she hollering. And button up your lip.

She didn't offer me coffee. She looked at me strictly all the time. I tried to look strictly back, but I failed because I loved the sight of her.

Donald was teary, but I didn't dare turn my face to him, until the parting minute at the door. Even then, I kissed the top of his head a little too forcefully and said, Well, I'll see you.

On the front stoop there were about half a dozen mid-morning family people and kids arguing about who had dumped garbage out of which window. They were very disgusted with one another.

Two young men in handsome dashikis stood in counsel and agreement at the street corner. They di-

vided a comment. How come white womens got rotten
teeth? And look so old? A young woman waiting at the
light said, Hush . . .

I walked past them and didn't begin my run till the
road opened up somewhere along Ocean Parkway. I
was a little stiff because my way of life had used only
small movements, an occasional stretch to put a knife
or teapot out of reach of the babies. I ran about ten,
fifteen blocks. Then my second wind came, which is
classical, famous among runners, it's the beginning of
flying.

In the three weeks I'd been off the street, jogging
had become popular. It seemed that I was only one person doing her thing, which happened like most American eccentric acts to be the most "in" thing I could
have done. In fact, two young men ran alongside of me
for nearly a mile. They ran silently beside me and
turned off at Avenue H. A gentleman with a mustache,
running poorly in the opposite direction, waved. He
called out, Hi, senora.

Near home I ran through our park, where I had
aired my children on weekends and late-summer afternoons. I stopped at the northeast playground, where I
met a dozen young mothers intelligently handling their
little ones. In order to prepare them, meaning no
harm, I said, In fifteen years, you girls will be like
me, wrong in everything.

At home it was Saturday morning. Jack had returned
looking as grim as ever, but he'd brought cash and a
vacuum cleaner. While the coffee perked, he showed
Richard how to use it. They were playing tick tack toe
on the dusty wall.

Richard said, Well! Look who's here! Hi!

Any news? I asked.

Letter from Daddy, he said. From the lake and water country in Chile. He says it's like Minnesota.

He's never been to Minnesota, I said. Where's Anthony?

Here I am, said Tonto, appearing. But I'm leaving.

Oh yes, I said. Of course. Every Saturday he hurries through breakfast or misses it. He goes to visit his friends in institutions. These are well-known places like Bellevue, Hillside, Rockland State, Central Islip, Manhattan. These visits take him all day and sometimes half the night.

I found some chocolate-chip cookies in the pantry. Take them, Tonto, I said. I remember nearly all his friends as little boys and girls always hopping, skipping, jumping and cookie-eating. He was annoyed. He said, No! Chocolate cookies is what the commissaries are full of. How about money?

Jack dropped the vacuum cleaner. He said, No! They have parents for that.

I said, Here, five dollars for cigarettes, one dollar each.

Cigarettes! said Jack. Goddamnit! Black lungs and death! Cancer! Emphysema! He stomped out of the kitchen, breathing. He took the bike from the back room and started for Central Park, which has been closed to cars but opened to bicycle riders. When he'd been gone about ten minutes, Anthony said, It's really open only on Sundays.

Why didn't you say so? Why can't you be decent to him? I asked. It's important to me.

Oh Faith, he said, patting me on the head because he'd grown so tall, all that air. It's good for his lungs. And his muscles! He'll be back soon.

You should ride too, I said. You don't want to get
mushy in your legs. You should go swimming once a
week.

I'm too busy, he said. I have to see my friends.

Then Richard, who had been vacuuming under his
bed, came into the kitchen. You still here, Tonto?

Going going gone, said Anthony, don't bat your eye.

Now listen, Richard said, here's a note. It's for Judy,
if you get as far as Rockland. Don't forget it. Don't
open it. Don't read it. I know he'll read it.

Anthony smiled and slammed the door.

Did I lose weight? I asked. Yes, said Richard. You
look O.K. You never look too bad. But where were
you? I got sick of Raftery's boiled potatoes. Where
were you, Faith?

Well! I said. Well! I stayed a few weeks in my old
apartment, where Grandpa and Grandma and me and
Hope and Charlie lived, when we were little. I took you
there long ago. Not so far from the ocean where Grandma made us very healthy with sun and air.

What are you talking about? said Richard. Cut the
baby talk.

Anthony came home earlier than expected that evening because some people were in shock therapy and
someone else had run away. He listened to me for a
while. Then he said, I don't know what she's talking
about either.

Neither did Jack, despite the understanding often
produced by love after absence. He said, Tell me again.
He was in a good mood. He said, You can even tell it
to me twice.

I repeated the story. They all said, What?

Because it isn't usually so simple. Have you known
it to happen much nowadays? A woman inside the

steamy energy of middle age runs and runs. She finds the houses and streets where her childhood happened. She lives in them. She learns as though she was still a child what in the world is coming next.

# GREAT NOVELS
# FROM THE LAUREL
# DISTINGUISHED CONTEMPORARY
# FICTION SERIES

☐ A FAIRY TALE OF NEW YORK *J. P. Donleavy* $1.75
  3233-03

☐ IN THE DAYS OF SIMON STERN *Arthur A. Cohen*
  $1.75 4342-09

☐ REVOLUTIONARY ROAD *Richard Yates* $1.75 7412-15

☐ THE BEASTLY BEATITUDES OF BALTHAZAR B.
  *J. P. Donleavy* $1.50 0471-18

☐ THE LAST PICTURE SHOW *Larry McMurtry* $1.25
  4674-23

☐ THE LYNCHERS *John Edgar Wideman* 95¢ 5086-06

☐ AUGUSTUS *John Williams* $1.50 1292-05

☐ A SINGULAR MAN *J. P. Donleavy* $1.50 7941-31

☐ THE CALL GIRLS *Arthur Koestler* $1.25 3176-02

☐ THE OGRE *Michael Tournier* $1.50 6730-04

☐ G *John Berger* $1.25 2757-01

## *Timely Books in Laurel Editions*

**IN SEARCH OF COMMON GROUND** ☐
Conversations with Erik H. Erikson and
 Huey P. Newton
*Introduced by Kai T. Erikson* 3769-05
The extraordinary record of two meetings between the noted
psychological theorist and the founder of the Black Panther
Party. $1.25

**WITHOUT MARX OR JESUS** ☐
The New American Revolution Has Begun
*Jean-François Revel* 9729-19
Expounds the conditions indispensable to a successful revolution
and provocatively points out how America uniquely fits this
bill. $1.25

**THE MASTER GAME** ☐
Beyond the Drug Experience
*Robert S. de Ropp* 5479-50
Explores the human psyche and details the specific techniques of
Creative Psychology through which man can achieve heightened
consciousness. $1.50

**THE CALL GIRLS** ☐
*Arthur Koestler* 3176-02
A frightening and funny novel which shows a group of aca-
demic "call girls" gathered to discuss mankind's chances for
survival as a microcosm of the very problems they are trying
to solve. $1.25

**Buy them at your local bookstore or use this handy coupon for ordering:**

| Dell | **DELL BOOKS**<br>**P.O. BOX 1000, PINEBROOK, N.J. 07058** |
|---|---|

Please send me the books I have checked above. I am enclosing $_____
(please add 25¢ per copy to cover postage and handling). Send check or
money order—no cash or C.O.D.'s.

Mr/Mrs/Miss_____

Address_____

City_____State/Zip_____

Hailed in *The New York Times* as
"first-rate, absorbing, informative,
judicious, and scholarly,"
here is the biography which exposes
the man behind the myth.

# LIVINGSTONE
## by Tim Jeal

Lauded by the Victorians as an explorer unrivaled since the
Elizabethans, Livingstone was revered as a near saint, epit-
omizing every moral virtue. The real man emerges as one
capable of ruthless cruelty, dogged throughout his life by
self doubts, contradictions and failure.

"This superb new biography differs from all previous ones in
its political and historical sophistication, and in its fidelity to
facts rather than sentiment."—*The New York Times Book
Review*

"Seems certain to be the standard biography of both man
and myth; it is hard to imagine why anyone need write the
story again."—*Smithsonian*

❧ **LAUREL EDITION** **$2.25** 4982-04